CRAZYBONE

Also by Bill Pronzini
in Large Print:

Boobytrap
Demons
Epitaphs
Firewind
Gallows Land
The Hangings
Jackpot
Quincannon
Sleuths
The Vanished
With an Extreme Burning
The Best Western Stories of Ed Gorman
The Texans: The Best of the West
The Gunfighters: The Best of the West
The Californians: The Best of the West
The Arizonans: The Best of the West

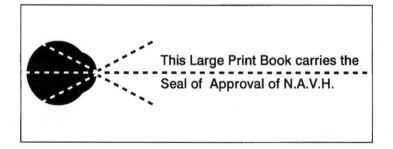

This Large Print Book carries the
Seal of Approval of N.A.V.H.

CRAZYBONE

A
"Nameless Detective"
Novel

Bill Pronzini

Thorndike Press • Thorndike, Maine

Published in 2000 by arrangement with Carroll & Graf
Publishers, Inc.

Thorndike Press Large Print Mystery Series.

The tree indicium is a trademark of Thorndike Press.

The text of this Large Print edition is unabridged.
Other aspects of the book may vary from the original edition.

Set in 16 pt. Plantin by PerfecType.

Printed in the United States on permanent paper.

Library of Congress Cataloging-in-Publication Data

Pronzini, Bill.
    Crazy bone : a nameless detective novel / by Bill Pronzini.
        p.   cm.
    ISBN 0-7862-2694-3 (lg. print : hc : alk. paper)
    1. Nameless Detective (Fictitious character) — Fiction.
2. Private investigators — California — San Francisco —
Fiction. 3. San Francisco (Calif.) — Fiction. 4. Large type
books. I. Title.
PS3566.R67 C7 2000
813'.54—dc21   00-055185

For the Poker Bunch —

Bette and J. J. Lamb
and
Peggy and Charlie Lucke

— Three Aces and a Wild Card

And special thanks to Bette Lamb
for medical assistance

1

Greenwood was a little pocket of the good life sewn into the low eastern slopes of the Santa Morena Ridge, on the peninsula about halfway between San Francisco and the smoggy sprawl of Silicon Valley. During Gold Rush times, it had been the only trading post in the region and was a gathering place for the lumberjacks and bullwhackers who worked the nearby sawmills. No lumberjack or bullwhacker could afford to work or shop there these days, much less live in the area. Nor could anyone else whose annual income ran below six figures.

Some years back a national magazine had described Greenwood's larger neighbor, Woodside, as a community "inhabited by gentlemen farmers, gentlemen ranchers, assorted exurbanites, and horses." The description suited Greenwood equally well. Mecca for the horsey set. Riding academies, commercial stables, a paddock or two on every block. Horses, in fact, were so prevalent and held in such regard that local laws had been enacted permitting easements across private property for bridle paths, and backyard stabling if a homesite was an acre or more. There was even an equine licensing tax.

It was the sort of place, despite its gentility and scenic attractions, that made me vaguely uncomfortable. I could never have lived there no matter how much money I had. Too snooty and white bread for my blood, lacking in ethnic mix. Besides which, the only interest I have in horses is now and then watching them run at Tanforan or Golden Gate Fields.

Still, I didn't mind a short visit on those rare occasions when a business matter took me down that way. Quiet there, unlike most other towns strung together along the Peninsula. Densely wooded slopes and hollows, pretty little creeks, gated and walled estates built with old money and maintained by new. The old-fashioned estates appeal to what Kerry and others have referred to as my dinosaur nature. Fortresslike stone houses and outbuildings, more than a few in the English Tudor style — anachronisms in the days of Y2K, relics of a time when nobody bothered to pretend that Americans live in a classless society. Not a better time; hell, no. But one I understood and identified with far more than the present day, when nearly everyone seems to have prostrated himself at the clay feet of the god Technology.

I turned off Highway 280 and rolled into Greenwood at two P.M. on a bright, crisp October afternoon. The town center was a country-village collection of the quaint and the modern: weathered wood and Spanish-style buildings even older than I am, cheek by jowl with tasteful little strip malls and a pseudo-rustic shopping center. The address I wanted turned out to be a two-story, tile-roofed, white stucco pile at least a century old, probably once a hotel and now a warren of professional offices. The one in which Richard Twining held sway was on the ground floor facing Greenwood Road, behind a chain-hung shingle that proclaimed *R. V. Twining — Insurance Services.*

Twining was waiting for me with a smile, a strong handshake, and a friendly clap on the shoulder. Pure salesman, and a good one to get away with a somewhat flashy presence in such a staid environment. He was about forty, blond, tanned, good-looking, dressed in knife-creased beige slacks, an expensive

9

navy-blue blazer, a silk shirt with the top two buttons undone, and a filigreed gold chain around his sunburned neck. An athlete once, I thought, still more or less in shape but with incipient jowls and the suggestion of a paunch. He had one of those deep, rumbly voices that some women consider an index to both masculinity and virility. The wedding ring on his left hand was three or four ounces of platinum gold and the private office he ushered me into was handsomely furnished. Doing all right for himself, R.V. was, in the insurance racket.

"Have a seat, make yourself comfortable," he said. "Coffee? Tea? Soft drink? Or I've got some really good twelve-year-old Scotch — "

"Nothing, thanks."

He sat down and leaned back in a padded leather armchair. "So. Frankly I don't know why Intercoastal would send an investigator out on a matter like this. I mean, you'd think they'd be happy about it and just let it slide."

"You've talked with Ken Fujita?"

"Oh, sure. But he wasn't exactly forthcoming, if you know what I mean. He confide in you?"

"Pretty much. How well do you know Ken?"

"Not very."

"Well, I've done some work for him in the

past. Inconsistent behavior in policy holders bothers him."

"Me, too, for that matter," Twining said. "But this case is just the opposite. How could there be any intent to defraud on Mrs. Hunter's part?"

"It's not that, it's the inconsistency itself. Why would anybody turn down fifty thousand dollars? That's what bothers Fujita."

"Pretty obvious, isn't it? She doesn't need the money. Jack Hunter left her well off."

"Not so well off, according to your report, that fifty thousand wouldn't be welcome. For her daughter's education, if nothing else. And why wouldn't she give you a specific reason? Why act the way she did?"

Twining scratched thoughtfully at his underlip. "I'll admit that makes me wonder, too. But I still don't see the need for an investigation. I could've worked on her myself to get the answers. No offense."

"None taken. There's another reason I was called in, the main one. Did Fujita discuss the publicity angle with you?"

"No. What publicity angle?"

"Intercoastal wants Mrs. Hunter to take the money," I said, "as a, quote, gesture of good will, unquote. Widow refuses payoff, compassionate insurance company convinces her to change her mind for the benefit of her family. It'll look good in the media and the head office, and brokers like you can milk it for new customers."

Twining wagged his head. Then he said, "You know, it's not a bad idea at that. Worth a lot more in the long run than the fifty K."

I said, "Uh-huh. But they don't want to push it until they're certain the Hunters are the all-American family they appear to be. No skeletons, nothing that can backfire on Intercoastal."

"And that's where you come in."

"Skeleton hunter, right. No pun intended."

"Okay, then. So how can I help?"

"Well, your report was pretty detailed, but I'd like to go over the specifics if you don't mind. Ask a few questions."

"No problem. Fire away."

"Let's start with the deceased. How well did you know Jackson Hunter?"

"Casually. We both played golf at Emerald Hills. That's where I signed him, in the bar at the country club." Twining grinned. "Nothing breaks down resistance like three or four martinis."

"Policy on his life only."

"Right. Term life, twenty-five thousand double indemnity. I tried to talk him into a joint spousal policy, but he wouldn't go for it.

12

He didn't even want Sheila — Mrs. Hunter — to know he'd taken out one on himself."

"Why, did he say?"

"Something about her hating the whole idea of insurance."

"You respected his wishes?"

"Sure. Customer is always right."

"This was, what, eighteen months ago?"

"About that."

"You see him much after you signed him?"

"Now and then. Casually, like I said."

"How did he seem to you? Stable, happy? Or a man with problems?"

"I'd say reasonably happy and rock-solid. Drank a little too much, but then, don't we all sometimes."

I let that pass. "Secure in his job?"

"Seemed to be. The computer racket can be iffy, but he wasn't a Silicon road runner. He — "

"Road runner?"

"Commuter, wage slave. Didn't work down in the Valley, at least not regularly. Private consultant, did most of his work at home. He'd been at it several years and he had a couple of medium-size companies on his client list."

"Estimated annual income?"

"Six figures, easy."

13

"A twenty-five-thousand-dollar double indemnity policy is pretty skimpy for a man making that kind of money."

"Exactly what I tried to tell him," Twining said. "He wouldn't listen. I had a hell of a time as it was, signing him on the small term life."

"Why do you think he bothered, then?"

"The truth?" Twining's grin this time was of the preening, self-congratulatory variety. "To get me off his back. Persistence is my middle name. I never met a sales resistance I couldn't break down sooner or later."

"I don't doubt that," I said. "No employment listing for Mrs. Hunter, I noticed."

"Nope. She didn't need to work, so she didn't."

"Was she trained for anything?"

Another grin, the smutty kind. He had quite a repertoire. "Women like Sheila don't need to be trained. She was born with all of her best skills."

"Meaning?"

"She's a fox," he said. "Genuine, grade-A stone fox. One of the most drop-dead gorgeous women I've ever set eyes on. Jack Hunter was one lucky bastard."

"Until two weeks ago, maybe. How does Mrs. Hunter . . . what's her maiden name, by the way? I didn't see it in the report."

"Underwood, I think."

I wrote that down. "How does she spend her time? Other than being a homemaker and mother, I mean."

"Potting, mostly. That's her thing."

"What kind of pottery?"

"Odd-shaped bowls and urns, bright glazes with black designs. Pretty good, if you like that kind of art. She has a studio behind their house."

"She sell or display any of her work?"

"Local gallery has a sampling for sale. Anita Purcell Fine Arts. Couple of blocks west of here on the main drag."

I made another note. "About the Hunters' marriage," I said then. "Would you say it was solid?"

"Who knows about things like that?" Twining said, and shrugged. "Looked good on the surface, especially where Jack was concerned. He talked about her all the time, all but drooled on her in public. So would I if I was married to a stone fox like that. Not that my wife's a dog, you understand."

Some compliment. I let that pass, too. "So as far as you know, they were faithful to each other."

"Depends on your definition of faithful. Me, I subscribe to the Clinton version." He laughed. "I can tell you this — she wouldn't

15

play the one time I tested the waters. And if I couldn't score, chances are nobody else could, either. Jack was the only one getting a piece of that pie."

Twining had succeeded in making me actively dislike him. He was one of the breed that looks at every woman the way a glutton looks at a plate of food; that measures and rates every woman in terms of her physical attributes, potential sexual prowess, and availability to him and his line of seductive bullshit. The type that thinks with his little head instead of his big one. A hard-on disguised as a man, in one of Kerry's more colorful phrases. Men like Richard Twining are a central reason why Betty Friedan and Gloria Steinem and the leaders of NOW became hardcore feminists. Difficult enough to take in their twenties and thirties, past forty their outlook and their shtick become pathetic as well as tiresome and annoying. As far as I was concerned, any woman who had the misfortune to be married to this horse's ass would be completely justified in having him gelded and stabled with the rest of Greenwood's aging stallions.

I managed to maintain an even tone when I asked, "What can you tell me about Mrs. Hunter's background?"

"From Pennsylvania, same as Jack.

16

Harrisburg. Married back there, moved out here when he got a job with Raytec in the Valley. I don't know anything about her family. Or his."

"They sound like private people."

"More so than most. Didn't talk much about themselves, and you couldn't draw them out."

"How long have they lived in Greenwood?"

"About ten years. Little girl, Emily, was born right after they settled here."

"Ever in trouble of any kind?"

"Model citizens," Twining said. "Kept to themselves, never bothered anybody." Elaborate sigh, followed by a broad wink. "I sure wish she'd let me bother her a time or two. Man, she — "

"Suppose we stick to the issue, Mr. Twining. I really don't care about your lust for Jack Hunter's widow."

He didn't like that. He opened his mouth, snapped it shut, glared at me for three or four seconds. I could almost read his thoughts: Tight-assed old fart. Maybe you're a fag, huh, buddy? It was a good thing for both of us that he kept them to himself.

There was no open declaration of hostility. Twining was first and foremost a salesman, whether it was insurance or himself he was peddling. And like it or not, I was a representative of one of the companies he worked for. His expression shape-changed until he was once again wearing his easygoing professional smile, a little more crooked now but otherwise firmly in place. It took about five seconds and it was like watching time-lapse photography of new skin knitting to erase a wound.

He said as if I hadn't interrupted him, "Two nice people, no question about that." His tone was cheerful; you had to listen close to hear the underlying anger.

"They have any close friends?"

"Not that I know about. Except maybe Doc Lukash. Jack played a lot of golf with him and I guess they were pretty friendly, at least at the club."

"Doc. Medical doctor?"

"Dentist. Lukash Dental Clinic, one of the largest in the county."

"Here in Greenwood?"

"Redwood City. Downtown, off El Camino."

I had him spell the name Lukash and then wrote it down in my notebook. "How about Mrs. Hunter? Anyone she sees fairly often — shopping, lunch? Or who shares her interest in potting?"

"Anita Purcell. Only one I know."

"Personal as well as business relationship?"

He dipped one shoulder; he didn't want to talk about Mrs. Hunter anymore. "You'd have to ask her."

"All right. Tell me about the accident."

"Not much to tell. One of those things. Jack went over to the coast on business, was driving home on Highway 84 about eight P.M. That's a mountain road, lots of twists and turns — "

"I know, I've driven it."

"Sure you have," Twining said. "Dark night, foggy, and he was heading up the grade out of La Honda. Damn drunk decided to pass a truck on the downhill side, misjudged the distance, hit Jack's car head on. Both of them killed instantly."

"No doubt that it was the drunk's fault?"

"None. Goddamn wetback off one of the farms out there. Booze-hounds, all those *braceros*, and menaces when they get behind the wheel."

Philanderer, chauvinist, and a bigot, too. I said thinly, "Drunk drivers come in all races, colors, and creeds."

"Yeah," he said. "What were you thinking? That maybe Jack committed suicide?"

"Always a possibility."

"He had no reason to kill himself."

"So you've indicated. How soon after the

19

accident did you talk to Mrs. Hunter about the policy?"

"Couple of days."

"You called her?"

"Called and then went to see her. Offer my condolences, get the paperwork started on the claim."

"And she didn't know anything about the policy."

"She did by then," Twining said. "Found it among Jack's papers. I asked her why she hadn't contacted me, and that was when she said she didn't want to file a claim, didn't want the fifty thousand."

"Do you remember her exact words?"

"'I don't need the money, I don't want it, Jack should never have taken out an insurance policy.' She just wanted to forget the whole thing."

"'Jack should never have taken out an insurance policy.' That's a funny way to phrase it."

"Funny?"

"As if he'd done something wrong."

"I guess she figured he had. She seemed pretty upset about it."

"Upset over a life insurance policy that would pay her and her daughter fifty thousand dollars. That just doesn't make a whole lot of sense."

Twining made a Who-knows? gesture with one hand. "She's one of those people who think insurance is a ghoul's game." He looked at me squarely and added, "Even stone-fox widows can be a little nuts."

I ignored it; there was nothing to be gained in challenging him again. "Did you talk to her after that?"

"Once. To see if maybe she'd changed her mind. She wouldn't even let me in the house."

"So you haven't told her about Intercoastal bringing in an investigator."

"Not my place. Besides, Fujita said I should keep it confidential. You going to see her?"

"As soon as I can."

"How about if I go out there with you, pave the way — "

"Not necessary. All I need is directions to her home."

He provided them, and we both came up out of our chairs as if some kind of bell had gone off. No handshake this time, no parting words — both of us anxious for me to be gone. At the door I glanced back and he gave a little dismissive wave; his smile had slipped halfway into a sneer. What an asshole, his eyes said.

I went out thinking the same about him.

2

One of the good things about living in Greenwood was that no matter where you were located, even along the main road through the village, you felt you were in the country. Trees and ground cover grew in dense profusion; half the streets and side roads were shade tunnels created by the interlocking branches of oak, manzanita, eucalpytus, plum and wild cherry, other trees I couldn't name. Busy six- and eight-lane Highway 280 was only a couple of miles away, but here the effect of quiet rusticity was so complete you might have been tucked away in a High Sierra back-water. To my mind, the best part was that it was still a natural habitat, not an architect's wet dream like so many ritzy planned communities these days. The builders had taken advantage of the environment without any sort of destructive tampering. Peaceful coexistence between man and nature. Every developer in California, particularly the perpetrators of tracts thrown up on indiscriminately clear-cut and bulldozed land, in which every house looks the same and the overall effect is of a gigantic penal colony, ought to be force-fed the principles of the Greenwood method.

But even then, I thought in my cynical fashion, the greedy bastards still wouldn't get it or give a damn if they did. They didn't care where or how other people lived, as long as they didn't have to be there among them. Half of the land-raping, build-'em-fast-and-loose developers in the Bay Area probably resided right here in woodsy, horsey, affluent Greenwood.

Whiskey Flat Road, along which I was driving as I indulged in these gloomy speculations, was a narrow lane about a third of a mile west of the village center, where the rolling land began to rise into steeper hills. There were homes on large parcels along both sides, a picture-postcard brook that kept meandering from one side of the road to the other through carefully constructed culverts. I passed gated drives, pastured horses, fences of wood and chainlink and stone and mossy brick, most of them overgrown with ivy or oleander shrubs. About half the houses were hidden, the rest partially so. Number 769 was more or less in the second category, set up on a little knoll on the west side and surrounded by trees and shrubbery so that you had a kind of filtered look at it even when you turned into the driveway. I couldn't even be sure of its architectural style from down below, though most of the Whiskey Flat homes were variations of the sprawling, single-story ranch type.

The drive was gated, but the gate was open; I went on through, uphill past the first screen of trees. Ranch-style, all right, off-white with dark-green trim, tinted glass and brickwork, solar panels, a redwood side deck that wrapped around to the rear; the whole cradled by two huge heritage oaks. The garage was detached, off on the right. On the far side stood a smaller outbuilding with a slanted glass roof, its near wall two-thirds glass. Sheila Hunter's potting studio.

I parked in a paved semicircle fronting the house. There were no other cars in sight, and when I rang the bell its chimes didn't bring anybody. I wandered over to the outbuilding. The afternoon sun threw flame-light off the glass surfaces, lit up the interior in a glaring way. The effect, as I approached, was of a building on fire. The woman in white sitting in the glass-walled section, motionless with her head bowed, might have been a penitent in some weird religious ceremony — or a corpse prepared for cremation in a glass oven.

The illusion vanished as I reached an open door in the wood-walled section. Unpleasant image, given the circumstances, and I was glad to be rid of it. I had a clearer look at the woman now; she was seated on a stool before a potter's wheel, her hands clasped between her knees, her back sharply bent forward and her head so far down I couldn't see her face behind a hanging screen of dark hair. The white outfit was a man's shirt and a pair of tailored jeans. No widow's weeds for Sheila Hunter, if that was who she was. Not that clothes make a grieving spouse; you can mourn just as deeply naked or in the raiments of royalty.

I poked my head through the doorway. "Mrs. Hunter?"

No answer. She didn't move, didn't seem to have heard me. I thought: Why not just go and leave her alone? But it was reflexive and without conviction. Like it or not, the nature of my job is to bother people, too often at the worst of times. If I started giving in to my overload of empathy, I might as well get out of the investigation business.

I stepped inside. Storage shelves of pots, bowls, urns in odd, twisted shapes, some wearing bright green and blue glazes overlain with geometric black designs, others unglazed. Tubs of wet clay. Miscellaneous clutter. A doorway without a door gave access to the glass-walled section where the woman sat. In there I could see a kiln, squatty and much tinier than I'd imagined kilns to be, and the potter's wheel and a long bench and not much else. I framed myself in the opening and said her name again. Still no response; she might've been in some kind of trance.

"Mrs. Hunter?" Louder, and a rap on the inner wall to go with it.

She came alive in a convulsive spasm, sitting bolt upright, the dark hair flying silkily as her head whipped around my way. For three or four seconds she gawped at me out of wide, bulging eyes — a look that made me recoil a little. It contained as much raw terror as I've ever seen in anyone's face. Then she was on her feet, in a movement so sudden it toppled the stool; backing away, one hand up in front of her as if she were trying to ward off an attacker. The edge of the workbench stopped her. She reached down to grab it with both hands, steadying herself, still radiating fear at me. Her eyes had an unfocused sheen. She was breathing so rapidly I thought she might start to hyperventilate.

"Crazybone," she said.

The word popped out in a thin, choked whisper. There was dread in it, and something else, a visceral emotion from deep within her. She seemed unaware of having spoken; it was a sleepwalker's word, a nightmare word.

I said, "I'm sorry, Mrs. Hunter, I didn't mean to frighten you."

"Oh, God." Eyeblinks, several of them. A palpable shudder. And then she was herself again, the eyes focusing, some of the terror retreating. "Who are you?" she said in a stronger voice. "What do you want?"

"I called to you twice from outside, but you — "

"Who *are* you?"

I told her my name, that I represented Intercoastal Insurance. I had one of my cards in hand, but I was afraid of setting her off again by approaching her with it. Instead I reached over and laid it on the clay-stained bench.

"Jesus," she said, "that fucking insurance policy." Then she said, "You scared the hell out of me, coming in here like that. You're trespassing."

"I'm sorry." I was tired of apologizing, but she was right on both counts. "Would you like me to come back at some other time?"

"Why? Why are you bothering me? I told Rich Twining I don't want to file a claim."

"Why not, Mrs. Hunter?"

"That's my business. Who sent you here? What do you do for Intercoastal Insurance?"

"I'm an independent investigator. I was hired to — "

"For God's sake!" The fear was back, a lurking presence that made her pale gray-green eyes almost luminous. She raised her hands to cup both elbows, pulling in tight against herself as if she were cold. "Investigating what? Me?"

"Not exactly. If you'll just let me explain — "

"I'm not going to file a damn claim. How much clearer do I have to make it to you people?"

"Would you turn down the fifty thousand dollars if it was given to you?"

"Given? What're you talking about?"

"Intercoastal deeply regrets your loss." Company line; I didn't believe it any more than she did. "As a gesture of goodwill to you and your daughter, they're willing to honor your husband's policy without the usual paperwork."

28

Incredulity crowded the fear aside. Twining had called her "drop-dead gorgeous," and there was justification for that assessment. Flawless complexion as luminous as her eyes, perfect features, that dark silken hair, a long-legged, high-breasted figure. But there was also a worn, haggard quality that diminished and roughened the edges of her beauty. Part of it was grief, no doubt, but it seemed more ingrained than that. The fear, maybe, a physical corrosive if you live with it long enough.

Pretty soon she said, "Why would they do a thing like that?"

"A gesture of goodwill, as I — "

"Oh, bullshit. Insurance companies don't give a damn about people. They don't do anything unless there's something in it for them."

"All right, Mrs. Hunter, I'll be candid. In return Intercoastal would ask the right to publicize their gesture, use your name in a promotional campaign."

"So that's it. My photograph, too, I suppose. And my daughter's name and photograph."

"With your permission, of course."

"I won't consent to anything like that. Never. What's the matter with them? I just lost my husband, Emily lost her father, our

29

lives are in a shambles. We're not about to become shills for a fucking insurance company."

"That's not what — "

"That's *exactly* what it is." She was angry now. The anger was genuine, but I had the impression she was working it up, using it to hold the fear at bay. "They hired you to poke around in my life, my husband's life, make sure we're not ax murderers or sexual deviants or something else that would make them look bad if it got out. Isn't that right?"

"There's nothing in your background you're ashamed of, is there?"

"Of course not!" She spat the words at me; the gray-green eyes flashed and sparked. "How dare you!"

"I didn't mean that to be insulting."

"I don't care what you meant. It is insulting, this whole ploy is insulting. You get out of here right now. You leave my daughter and me alone, stay out of our lives. And you tell your bosses if they bother me again in any way I'll sue them for harassment. You understand?"

"Yes, ma'am, I understand."

"Now get off my property. And don't come back."

I didn't argue with her; it would have been an indefensible argument even if I'd had the inclination. All I did was nod and walk out into the sunlight and tree shadows. She followed me as far as the studio entrance. When I glanced back after a time she was still standing there, still hugging herself as if there was no more warmth in the day and little enough in her body.

As I came around the nearest of the big oaks into the parking circle, I saw that my car had a visitor. A slender little girl of nine or ten stood on its near side, peering at it the way you would at a giant and unfamiliar bug.

She turned her head when she heard me approaching, and her posture changed into a kind of poised wariness like a cat's when it sees a stranger — not startled, not afraid, but ready to run if the situation called for it. I smiled and slowed my pace, but if that reassured her any, she didn't show it. Even though she was motionless, facing me as I came up, she still gave the impression of being on the verge of flight. No, not flight exactly. Up close, it seemed more like a readiness to retreat, to take refuge within herself. A defense mechanism of the shy, the vulnerable, the lonely.

"Hello," she said. She made eye contact all right and her voice was cordial, but she seemed uncomfortable, as if she wished one of us wasn't there. "Who are you?"

"Nobody special. Insurance man, I guess you could say."

"Oh."

"You're Emily?"

She nodded. "Is my mom in her studio?"

"Yes. I tried to talk to her, but she told me to go away."

A little silence. Then, "She doesn't like it that Daddy took out a policy."

"Why is that, Emily?"

"I don't know. Did you know my father?"

"No, I never met him."

"I miss him," she said.

It might have been an awkward moment. What do you say to a ten-year-old who has suddenly and tragically lost her father? But her words were a simple, solemn declaration that required nothing of me, least of all pity. Emily Hunter had to be hurting inside, but her pain was a private thing to be shared with no one except her mother. She resembled Sheila Hunter physically — the same fine, dark hair and luminous eyes and willowy body — but I sensed an emotional stability in her that was lacking in her mother. Self-contained, better equipped to handle a crisis, mature beyond her years.

"What will you and your mom do now?" I asked. "Will you stay here, do you think?"

"It's our home. We don't have anywhere else to go."

"No relatives back in Pennsylvania?"

"Where?"

"Pennsylvania. Harrisburg. Your folks are from there, aren't they?"

"There's just us," Emily said, and I couldn't tell if it was an evasion or not. "Except for Aunt Karen, but she — "

She broke off abruptly, as if she'd been about to say something she wasn't supposed to. It prompted me to ask, "Where does your aunt Karen live?"

Emily shook her head: closed subject. "We have enough money so we'll never have to worry. We don't need the money from Dad's insurance policy."

Parroting words of her mother's, I thought. "I'm glad to hear that," I said. "But people can always use a little extra, in case of emergency."

"No. Mom said — "

"Emily!"

We both turned. Sheila Hunter was striding toward us, almost running. Even at a distance I could see the tenseness in her body, the anger that put splotches of dark blood in her face.

She came up fast, her breath rattling a little, and said, "Emily, go into the house,"

33

without looking at her daughter. The glaring hostility was all for me.

"Mom, I — "

"Right now. You heard me, go."

Emily aimed an unreadable glance at me, then went straight to the front door and inside. No hesitation, no backward look. As if she were escaping rather than obeying.

"You," the woman said to me, the way you'd say it to a dog you'd just caught relieving itself in your front yard. "What do you think you're doing?"

"Your daughter was here when I came out. We were just talking."

"You were trying to pump her for information. What did she tell you?"

"Nothing. What're you afraid she might have told me?"

"Damn you! I told you to leave us alone! If you're not gone in one minute I'll call the police and report you. I mean it, one minute."

I was in the car and rolling in less than thirty seconds. And bidding a none too fond good-bye to Greenwood ten minutes after that. End of a brief and unsatisfactory visit to the Peninsula's lap of luxury. End of job, too, right? Sheila Hunter wouldn't take Intercoastal's fifty K if they brought it to her in small, unmarked, tax-free bills; Inter-

34

coastal could not capitalize on her and her daughter's tragedy no matter how squeaky clean the Hunters might be; so there was no point in continuing my investigation. Go back to the office, write up a report for Tamara to feed into her computer and send to Ken Fujita, and then move on to the next case on the docket.

Except that I did not want to let go of this one just yet.

I kept thinking about the little inconsistencies and ambiguities that had cropped up during my conversations with Sheila and Emily Hunter. I kept getting mental glimpses of the woman's fear and wondering what could generate such abnormal terror in a recent widow. And I kept hearing the word that had popped out of her when she'd first seen me, the nightmare word "crazybone."

A reasonable amount of curiosity is a good thing for a private investigator to have; too much, though, becomes a drawback. I had way too damn much. Always had, always would. And along with it, an overactive imagination and a need to find answers. The combination had gotten me in trouble more than once, so you'd think I would have learned from past experience. You'd be wrong. In spite of myself I kept right on giving in to my weaknesses, making the same mistakes — doing it my way, just like Old Blue Eyes.

So I wouldn't write a report to Ken Fujita yet. A little more digging first, maybe some answers that would satisfy me even if they were irrelevant to Intercoastal Insurance. And at my expense, since I couldn't justify putting it on their tab.

Crazybone. Hell, it was a word you could use to describe my head.

3

On my way out of Greenwood I passed Anita Purcell Fine Arts. I would have gone in there to talk to the Purcell woman except that the place was dark and there was a Closed sign in the window. I swung into the lot long enough to read a smaller sign that said their hours were eleven to five, Thursday through Sunday.

In Redwood City I stopped at a service station and looked up the address for the Lukash Dental Clinic. It turned out to be an operation large enough to warrant its own building, a refurbished pile that took up a third of a block on a downtown side street. Busy place. The parking lot was packed, and inside, the reception area contained four uncomfortable-looking individuals waiting on chairs and two women working phones and appointment calendars behind a horse-shoe desk. Other people wandered in and out while I was there, hygienists and dentists in white smocks and patients who were all done being drilled and scraped and polished and X-rayed. Nobody seemed particularly happy except the staff; they all smiled a lot, maybe to demonstrate that they practiced what they preached, since every one of them had very white teeth. Or maybe they were cheerful because they were integral cogs in what was obviously a successful assembly line production.

The older of the horseshoe women said yes, Dr. Lukash was in, but at the moment he was tending to an emergency patient. She imparted this information with a kind of hushed gravity, as if whatever his ministrations might be, they were a matter of life and death. Would he be available within the next half hour to discuss a personal matter? She thought he might be, so I wrote the words "Regarding Sheila Hunter" on the back of one of my cards and passed it over. She looked at the printed front, lost her smile and peered at me with sudden suspicion, then went away stiffly with her lips compressed. Some people view private detectives with the same jaundiced eye as they do process servers, bill collectors, and IRS auditors — as harbingers of calamity, trouble on the hoof.

I sat on a thin-cushioned chair to wait. The woman came back and busied herself again without looking at me; as far as she was concerned, I wasn't there and never had been, like Yehudi. I thumbed through a copy of *Sports Illustrated* and watched the ebb and flow and listened to the sinister whine of drills from hidden cubicles.

After eighteen minutes by the clock behind the horseshoe, a tall, white-coated party put in an appearance. He consulted with the receptionist, then came over to me. He was in his early forties, going gray around the edges in a distinguished fashion; his thick mane had the kind of wave in it that said he frequented a men's styling salon instead of a barbershop. He didn't have a smile for me, since I was not a paying customer, so I couldn't tell much about his teeth until we started talking. I made a bet with myself that they would be even whiter and more perfect than his staff's — an easy winner.

He introduced himself as Dr. Arthur A. Lukash and then said, "We'll talk in my office. I can give you about five minutes." Crisp and civil, nothing more or less. Without waiting for a response, he turned and walked back across the reception area. It was not much of a slight, but just enough for me to work up a mild dislike for him as I trailed along behind.

His office was small and cramped and smelled as if it had been swabbed down with antiseptic. "Now then," he said as he lowered his backside into a desk chair, "what's this about Sheila Hunter? I can't imagine a detective has any reason to bother the poor woman. Or me, for that matter."

I explained who had hired me and why. I didn't say anything about my confrontation with Mrs. Hunter.

Lukash said, "It was my understanding she had no interest in Jack's insurance."

"Intercoastal hopes to change her mind."

"Not to the point of harassing her, I trust."

"Of course not."

"The fact is, Sheila . . . Mrs. Hunter is a strong-willed woman. Once she has made up her mind, no one is likely to change it."

"She and her daughter are entitled to the insurance money. Why do you suppose she's so set against it?"

"I have no idea." He put his hands together and the points of his fingers under his chin, a prayerlike gesture that struck me as habitual. Pretty soon he said, "Just why are you here? I don't see what I can possibly tell you."

"I spoke with Richard Twining earlier; he said you and Jack Hunter were friends. I thought you might — "

"He told you wrong. Jack and I were not friends."

"But you did know him fairly well?"

"Wrong again. I played golf with the man, I occasionally socialized with him and his wife at the club, but I neither knew him well nor exchanged confidences with him. I doubt anyone other than Sheila knew Jack well."

"Meaning he was private, hard to know."

"Closed off, yes. He shut everyone out except his family."

"That sounds as though you didn't much like him."

"I didn't dislike him," Lukash said. "He was a casual acquaintance, that's all. I was sorry to hear about the accident, but more sorry, frankly, for Sheila and Emily."

"How well do you know Mrs. Hunter?"

He stiffened. "What do you mean by that?"

The sudden wary defensiveness in his voice prompted me to ask, "What do you think I mean, Doctor?"

"I don't know her any better than I knew Jack."

"Another casual acquaintance."

41

"That's right." His mouth worked as if he were trying not to scowl. "Did Rich Twining say something to you about Sheila and me?"

"Such as what?"

"He did, didn't he. Dammit, he's the one with a lech for her. Did he tell you that?"

"He didn't make any bones about it," I said.

"He's a liar if he told you he slept with her. She wouldn't have anything to do with him and it offends his ego."

I let that pass without comment.

Lukash said, "I'll bet he didn't mention Trevor Smith's name."

"Who would Trevor Smith be?"

"I thought not. He can't stand the idea that Smith could succeed where he couldn't."

"You haven't told me who Smith is."

"The club pro at Emerald Hills."

"Golf pro? The Greenwood Country Club?"

"Yes."

"He and Mrs. Hunter are involved, is that what you're saying? Had an affair or are still having one?"

"Don't put words in my mouth," Lukash said priggishly. "I don't tell tales, I'm not Rich Twining."

"And you have nothing to hide."

"Nothing whatsoever. My relations with Sheila Hunter have always been strictly aboveboard. I am not in the habit of playing around with tramps."

"Tramps, Doctor? Is that what Mrs. Hunter is?"

Lukash clamped thin lips over his pretty white teeth. He'd said too much and was already starting to regret it. He glanced pointedly at his watch and then got to his feet, saying, "Your five minutes are up." He looked at a spot past my left ear and added, "I'll thank you not to bother me again. Or to repeat anything that has been discussed here. If you do — "

"I don't carry tales, either, Doctor," I said, and left him standing there looking pretty damn guilty for a man who had nothing to hide.

It was five-thirty by the time I got back into the city and up to my office. Tamara was long gone; Tuesday is generally one of her half days, because of classes at San Francisco State. On my desk was a note from her — computer printout, of course, since she never wrote anything by hand if she could help it. Child of the new age. Two phone messages, neither of any importance, and a cryptic one-liner that read: "Still

43

working on the Hunter bg check but what I've got so far is VERY interesting." The "VERY" was not only in large caps but one of those fancy curlicue typefaces computers can print up these days.

So what did this mean? Sheila Hunter was already a complex little enigma: uninterested in an easy fifty thousand dollars, terrified of something, as closed off as her late husband, possibly an unfaithful wife. More than that, too? The owner of some dark, VERY interesting secret tucked away in her and/or her late husband's background?

I sighed. Tamara Corbin is an efficient young woman, but she has yet to lose her flair for the dramatic. When she does, and when she has a few more years of experience, she'll make a twenty-first-century detective to put to shame a technophobic twentieth-century dinosaur like me. Most of the time the prospect pleases me; having a protégé with unlimited potential gives me a sense of accomplishment. Occasionally, though, considering her intelligence, ambition, organizational and computer skills, and indispensability after only two years of part-time effort, I wonder if maybe the real protégé in the agency is its founder. And then I just feel old.

There was one message on the answering

machine, which Tamara had switched on before leaving; also not important. Other messages might well be waiting on e-mail, along with whatever Tamara's background check on the Hunters had uncovered, but since I didn't know and refused to be taught how to access anything on the new office computer, I'd have to wait for tomorrow. Old, yes. And stubborn and outmoded, with a crazybone for a head.

I locked up again and took my hidebound hide home to the one other woman on the planet besides Tamara with the patience to put up with me — and the only one with the understanding, compassion, courage, and sheer masochism to marry me and let me share her bed.

Kerry said, "We need to talk."

Uh-oh, I thought. I had been home exactly twelve seconds, just enough time for her to give me a quick kiss and me to give Shameless a quick pat. Home being her condo on Diamond Heights, where we spent most of our time together — to the point where I was actually thinking of giving up my Pacific Heights flat, even though it was rent-controlled and I'd had it for nearly thirty years. Sentimentality only goes so far, even with me. Simple fact was, the flat was no longer home to me and the condo was.

I straightened as the cat continued to wind himself around my legs, making his fluttery little motorboat noise. "Talk about what?"

"Cybil. I spoke to her a little while ago."

"She all right?"

"She says she is. I don't think so."

"Not some kind of health problem?"

"No, thank God."

"Trouble with her new novel?"

"Not that, either. Something's going on over there."

Cybil was Kerry's eighty-year-old mother. "Over there" was Redwood Village, a seniors' complex in Marin County where Cybil had lived the past two years. In the forties and fifties she'd been a successful writer for the pulp magazines, mainly of stories about a hardboiled detective named Samuel Leatherman. She had abandoned fiction writing when the pulps folded, and taken it up again after a forty-year hiatus when she moved to Redwood Village. You'd think she might have lost some of her skills after such a long layoff, but not if you knew Cybil. She had not only written her first novel and sold it to one of the smaller New York publishers, she'd been given a contract for a sequel.

I said, "What do you mean, going on?"

"At Redwood Village."

"You mean with the staff? One of her neighbors?"

"I'm not sure. But it might be serious."

"What makes you say that?"

"I think she wants to hire you to investigate whatever it is."

"What? Oh, come on — "

"I'm not kidding. She didn't come right out and say so, but she hinted around about it."

"Didn't she give you any idea of what it is?"

"Just that it has something to do with Archie Todd. You remember him, the retired ferryboat captain who lived across from her."

We were in the kitchen now, procuring a beer for me and a glass of wine for Kerry. I took a long swig of Bud Light before I said, "What about Captain Archie?"

"He died suddenly last week. I got the impression Cybil believes it may not have been of natural causes."

"Suicide?"

"Or homicide."

I had another long pull. "In a place like Redwood Village? Who would want to kill a nice old bird like Captain Archie?"

"Don't ask me."

"How did he die?"

"She didn't say. She wants us to come to lunch on Saturday and she'll talk to us about it then."

"What did you tell her?"

"I said we'd come. I thought you'd be as curious as I am."

"Sure, curious. But if she actually does want to hire me . . . My God, she's got me confused with Samuel Leatherman."

"You can listen to what she has to say, can't you? It's not like you're under any obligation to her."

"I didn't mean I wouldn't listen. I only meant — "

"Keep an open mind and then do what you think best," Kerry said. "She really is upset about whatever happened to Captain Archie. I could hear it in her voice. And Cybil is more level-headed than either of us, you know that. If she thinks something funny's going on, then something probably is."

"Okay, okay. If there's anything I can do for her, you know I will."

We took our drinks into the living room and settled into our Mom and Pop chairs. But I didn't get to enjoy the rest of my beer. Kerry saw to that.

"There's something else we have to discuss," she said.

"Uh, what?"

"Friday night. The cocktail party at Bates and Carpenter. I told you about it last week, remember?"

A little worm of premonition began to crawl slimily among the hairs on my neck. "I remember," I said warily. "What about it?"

"I know how much you hate large social gatherings, but — "

"Oh God."

" — but I need you to go with me."

"No," I said. "No way."

"It's important. To me, to the agency, and to Anthony DiGrazia. I wouldn't ask you if it wasn't."

"DiGrazia?"

"Don't play dumb. I told you about him, too. My new account — DiGrazia's Old-Fashioned Italian Sausages. The party is in his honor, to celebrate his signing with B and C."

"All right, so?"

"He's as old-fashioned as his sausages. Family values and all that. Married couples are supposed to attend social functions together, get acquainted with one another's spouses — especially when the function is business-related. Plus, he knows who you are, he's read about you in the papers. He wants to meet his 'fellow paisan.' Jim Carpenter thinks — I think — he'll be offended if you're not at the party, no matter what the excuse."

I didn't say anything. Shameless jumped up on my lap and began digging his claws into my knee. I glared at him and said to Kerry, "How about if we take the cat along, too? One big happy family for old Anthony to get to know."

"Oh, cut it out," she said. "It's one evening out of your life. Do I ask things like this of you very often?"

"All right," I said.

"Well? Do I?"

"No. I said all right. How many people will be there?"

"Seventy-five or so."

I managed not to cringe. "How long will it last?"

"Just a couple of hours. Five to seven. And dinner after that, but it'll only be six of us — the DiGrazias, Jim and his current lady, you and me."

"Sounds like fun," I said. Sounds like a slice of hell, I thought.

"Don't be sarcastic."

"I wasn't being sarcastic," I lied. "Don't worry, I'll be on my best behavior and I'll try

50

to have a good time. Anything for you, my love."

"Mmmmm," she said. One of those sounds women make that call to mind the warning rattle of a diamondback. Meaning I'd better be on my best behavior and I'd better try very hard to have a good time. Or else. Just what the "or else" might be, I preferred not to speculate.

4

Tamara was twenty-five minutes late on Wednesday morning. When she showed up she wore a quirky little smile and a satisfied, cat-in-the-cream expression. I knew that look; I'd had it myself on more than one occasion.

"That Horace," she said as she hung up her favorite grungy coat. "Have to be changing his name to Mr. Sun pretty soon."

"Mr. Sun?"

"Up bright and early, just keeps getting hotter and hotter. Too many mornings like this, I'm gonna have to start wearing sunblock to bed."

"Tell me something, Ms. Corbin," I said. "Why is it young people feel compelled to discuss their sex lives in such great detail?"

"Why not? Sex is cool, man." She grinned. " 'Specially when it's hot."

"It's also private, or should be."

"Well, we don't have hangups about doing the nasty."

"Who's 'we'? Generation X?"

"Lot more open than yours, right?"

"Too open, if you ask me."

"No such thing. Better to call it sweet and clean than pretend it's dirty. Besides, don't you remember how it was?"

"How what was?"

"Bein' my age. Horny all the time instead of every once in a while."

"What does that mean? Every once in a while?"

"You know, now and then."

"Define 'now and then.'"

"Birthdays, holidays, like that."

"Is that what you think? People in their fifties and sixties only have sex on birthdays and holidays, if they have it at all? Seven or eight times a year?"

"That often? I figured maybe two or three."

". . . Are you putting me on?"

"No, sir. Horace's folks don't do it at all anymore. That's what his daddy told him and he's only fifty-two."

"That's too bad. But for your information, Ms. Corbin, some of us old codgers still manage to indulge regularly. Not as regularly as you and Horace, God knows, but as often as once or twice a week."

"Lordy."

"In the morning, the afternoon, and sometimes even more than once a day. Not always in the missionary position, either, contrary to what you probably believe."

She made a "tsk" sound and shook her head. "Tell me something, boss," she said, deadpan. "Why is it middle-aged people feel compelled to discuss their sex lives in such great detail?"

I stared at her for about three seconds and then burst out laughing. She'd been putting me on, all right, playing me the way Horace, her symphonically inclined boyfriend, plays his cello. Score another one for Tamara. Trying to win a point, any point, with her was like going one-on-one against Michael Jordan. You didn't stand a chance; she had too many moves and too much quickness, and every time you ended up feeling out-maneuvered and overmatched.

"Okay," I said when I got my face straight again, "let's do some work here. You can start by explaining that cryptic note you left me yesterday."

"About the Hunters? *Very* interesting stuff, so far."

"So you said. Interesting how?"

"Mr. Jackson Hunter in particular. Seems

the man was ten and a half years old when he died."

"What?"

"Intercoastal application says he was born in Harrisburg, P.A., in 1960," Tamara said. "I checked the Vital Stats Bureau there. No birth record for anybody named Jackson Hunter. Not that year and not any year between fifty-five and sixty-five."

"One of the nearby towns . . ."

"Uh-uh. Pennsylvania's not a big state, so I checked all the counties. A few Jackson Hunters and Jack Hunters, but they're all the wrong race, deceased prior to two weeks ago, or still living in P.A."

Frowning, I said, "Sheila Hunter is supposed to be from Harrisburg, too. Twining told me her maiden name is Underwood."

"Yeah, I got that from the daughter's birth record. No Sheila Underwood born in Harrisburg during that same ten-year span. And there be no record of a Hunter-Underwood marriage."

"All right. But that doesn't make Jack Hunter ten and a half years old when he died. How'd you come up with that figure?"

"Man's Social Security number," Tamara said. "Can't get any information out of the Social Security Administration — be easier to hack into the Pentagon files — but the number itself tells you some things. First three digits, where it was issued. Other digits, approximately when."

"And Hunter's was issued ten and a half years ago."

"Yep. In New York City."

"Mrs. Hunter?" Her Social Security number was on the application, too.

"Same time, same place."

"So. Brand-new IDs for both of them."

"Told you it was interesting stuff. What d'you think? Fugitives, maybe?"

"Maybe. People with something to hide, in any event. The daughter's birth record tell us anything?"

"Not much. Born October 16, ten years ago. Peninsula Hospital, Redwood City."

"October 16th is tomorrow."

"Yeah," Tamara said.

I shook my head, wondering if the fact that Sheila Hunter had been pregnant when the two of them moved to Greenwood had anything to do with the identity switch. It was possible. Hell, anything was possible in a shuffle like this.

"Did you check on their house purchase?" I asked. "I'd like to know when they bought it and how they managed to get a loan."

"Didn't need a loan," Tamara said. "They paid cash."

"Cash? For real estate in Greenwood?"

"Four hundred thousand. No loan ap, no references, just a clean cash deal."

"When?"

"Seven years ago. First three years, they rented."

"They didn't buy the house with a bagful of bills. Even drug traffickers are smarter than that."

"Transfer of funds from an L.A. bank. No way I can trace where they be coming from before that. If they got the money from selling another piece of property, they didn't own it under the Hunter or Underwood names, least not in California. Probably not New York, either, but I'll check."

"Do that."

"Could be a high-end real estate scam," she said musingly. "Have to have new IDs after a deal like that."

"Or some other kind of big-money scam. Or the cash could've come from any of a couple of dozen legal or quasi-legal sources." I got up to pour myself another cup of coffee. "Twining told me Hunter worked for Raytec in Silicon Valley when he first came to Greenwood. Maybe his employment files can tell us something."

She made that "tsk" sound again. "Be

illegal for me to hack into a company's personnel files."

"I know it and I wouldn't ask you to. This is my kind of job — the dinosaur approach."

I looked up the number for Raytec Corporation in the Santa Clara County phone directory, one of a dozen Bay Area books we keep in the office. They had an automated telephone system, which meant I had to go through a lot of button-pushing nonsense before I got to talk to a real live human being in the personnel department. I gave my name and the agency name without including the word "detective," and said more or less truthfully that I was the CEO; then I said a Mr. Jackson Hunter had applied for a position with us in our computer department, giving Raytec as a former-employee reference. What could they tell me about him? Sometimes when you work this ploy, they'll ask for a telephone number so they can call you back to verify you're who you claim to be. The woman at Raytec was more trusting than most; she put me on hold while she communed with her computer.

"I'm sorry, sir," she said a couple of minutes later, "but your applicant seems to have given you false information. Raytec has never employed a Jackson or Jack Hunter in any capacity."

I relayed this to Tamara after I hung up. She said, "Not much of a surprise, huh?"

"Not much. Either he worked for them under another name, or he picked Raytec out of the blue as part of his cover. Little chance of him getting caught in the lie unless he used Raytec as an actual reference."

Tamara considered before she said, "Have to give some kind of reference to get a private consultancy job. No company'd hire him without a pretty solid one. You know which companies he was supposed to've done business with?"

"No, except that one might be on the coast — Half Moon Bay, most likely. Hunter was coming back from a business meeting, apparently, when he was killed. Richard Twining might be able to supply the name."

But when I got Twining on the phone he said, "I don't remember Jack ever mentioning the outfits he worked for. Why don't you ask Sheila?"

Which would be wasted effort, after yesterday's little run-in. No point in calling Doc Lukash, either; even if he'd talk to me I doubted he would have any more information than Twining.

"Know what I think?" Tamara said. "Man didn't work as a consultant for any company. Wasn't in the industry at all. Phony employment background for his new ID."

"That's what I'm thinking, too. But then where he'd get the money to buy his house? And to maintain an affluent lifestyle for three people for so many years?"

"Shaping up into some big mystery, huh?"

"Yeah," I said. "And I wonder just how deep it goes."

I called Ken Fujita at Intercoastal and laid the whole thing out for him. I said I could have a final report on his desk by the end of the week, but he said no, hold off and stay on the case a while longer at Intercoastal's expense, see if I could get to the bottom of it.

"You've saved us money and embarrassment already," he said, "so you're entitled to the extra benefit. Besides, I'm as curious about the Hunters as you are. Whatever you find out about this game of theirs may help us build in safeguards against potential fraud."

Insurance companies are unpredictable and often enough they make decisions that surprise you, but the decisions that involve largesse for employees are rare. Two in a row from Intercoastal was akin to finding a celibate politician in Washington. Not that this one was altruistic, any more than the original one of paying off Jack Hunter's term life policy had been; something in it for them, as always. Still, it restored some of my faith in the quid pro quo of business dealings — the straightforward approach that seems to have been eroded by incompetence, greed, disinterest, and irresponsibility, and become the exception rather than the norm. The "do a good job and you'll be rewarded for it" concept.

I said as much to Tamara. She said, "Retro, man. Things don't work that way anymore, from the top on down. All the corporate dudes care about is P for Profit, and screw everybody else. Bound to infect the rest of us."

"You can't have much profit without hard work."

"Sure you can. Screwing's easier and brings the money in faster."

"So what're you saying? Big Business screws us, so it's all right for us to screw them in return? And anybody else on a lower rung, right on down to the bottom?"

"New quid pro quo, boss. Business, politics, you name it. That's how the world operates these days."

"Brave new world."

"More like Orwell's than Huxley's."

"That your philosophy, too, college girl?

Get all you can for the least amount of effort? Look out for Number One and nobody else? Screw your way through life?"

"Well," she said, "the more you do the nasty, the better you get at it and the better off you are."

The words came through one of her wry little grins, so I was reasonably sure she was kidding. I hoped she was. What little promise I hold for the future is wrapped up in intelligent young people like Tamara Corbin — the kind of person I believed she was at heart. The possibility that I was nothing more to her than somebody to use on her way up the ladder was too depressing to even consider.

Other business took me away from the office for the rest of the morning and part of the afternoon. It was three o'clock when I returned. Tamara was industriously thumping away on her new Mac G3. She hadn't been able to come up with anything else about the Hunters, she said, so she'd moved on to the Holloway case, a missing-husband trace that she was making headway on.

The phone rang not long after I sat down. Tamara was still busy, so I picked up. And a small, strong voice said without hesitation, "This is Emily Hunter. Are you the man

62

who came to see my mother yesterday?"

I said yes, I was, managing to keep the surprise out of my voice. "What can I do for you, Emily?"

"Well, I found your business card in her studio. That's how I knew your phone number. She doesn't know I'm calling you."

"I see."

"She wouldn't like it if she did."

"I won't tell her. All my calls are confidential."

"Thank you," she said. Very grave and serious, even more so than yesterday. With something added that I took to be a kind of worried determination. "Could I talk to you? In person, I mean."

"Of course you can. It must be important."

"It is."

"Something about your mother?"

"Yes."

"What's making her so afraid?"

Pause. "I can't talk about it now. She might come in any minute. Tomorrow, okay? After school?"

I glanced at my calendar; the afternoon was free. "Anytime you say. Where would you like to meet?"

"Do you know the Rincon Riding Academy?"

"No, but I'm sure I can find it."

"It's on Rincon Road. Not far from where I live. I take riding lessons there every Thursday at three-thirty. We could meet in front at a quarter after."

"Quarter after three it is."

Another pause. I could hear the faint raspy sound of her breathing, the underlying tension in it. Then, "I have to talk to somebody. There's no one else. I don't know anyone else."

"I understand. I'll help if I can."

"Thank you," she said again. She started to say something else, broke it off; then, quickly, "Good-bye."

"Good-bye, Emily." But she had already severed the connection.

I put the receiver down, thinking: It cost her a lot to make that call. She isn't the kind of kid who asks for help easily, particularly not from a stranger. Whatever's going on there, she's caught in the middle. Dead father, terrified mother, and neither of them who they've pretended to be. Does she know who her parents really are, that she's been living a lie herself?

All of that, and tomorrow's her tenth birthday.

Jesus, what some people do to their children!

5

Back in horse country again. Parked in front of the Rincon Riding Academy, waiting for Emily Hunter, watching the activity in the block-square complex. Horses everywhere — horses on my mind.

Noble steed. Cayuse, bronc, bangtail, hayburner, crowbait. Grace and speed on a racetrack; maker and loser, all unknowing, of bettors' fortunes. Work animals, like cattle and oxen. Companion animals, same pet class as cats and dogs according to the proponents of a victorious proposition on last year's state ballot to "recognize horses as an important part of California's heritage that deserve protection from those who would slaughter them for food for human consumption." Steaks, chops, and roasts to the unfussy palates of Europeans and Japanese, the main markets for horsemeat. Even a taxidermist's delight — Roy

Rogers' taxidermist anyway.

Horses are a lot of different things to a lot of different people, to some of them passionately so, but I was not one of the multitude. Strictly neutral on the subject, although I'd voted for the proposition because I don't like to see any animal suffer inhumane treatment for any reason. Horses themselves, though, I can take or leave alone and mostly I prefer the latter. For one very good reason.

The noble steed is a smelly bugger.

Proof of this was borne on the warm afternoon breeze, a pungent combination of manure, urine, sweat, dust, and harness leather from the twenty or so cayuses boarded at the Rincon Riding Academy. It wasn't altogether unpleasant; the problem with it was pervasiveness. The smell got inside your nose and sinus cavities and stayed there. The horsey set obviously didn't mind, probably got so used to the aroma after a while they didn't even notice it. I always noticed it, even at a distance; up close and personal it was twice as potent. I hoped Emily wouldn't want me to go inside the cavernous riding barn with her. If I had to do that, the scent of horse would not only go home with me but would no doubt linger for some time. Even Kerry would smell like a

Kentucky Derby candidate, which would severely inhibit our sex life . . .

A young girl on a bicycle came along the road from the opposite direction and turned in at the academy's gate. Emily's size and age, but not Emily. I glanced at my watch. Almost twenty past three. She was a little late, not that that had to mean anything.

I shifted position and thought about putting the window up. Wouldn't have done much good; the equine effluvium had taken up residence inside the car. Besides, it was a warm day and I liked the feel of the breeze on my face.

Half a dozen kids and an older woman, all of them in riding togs and mounted on black-and-brown horses, filed out of the barn into an outdoor arena. I watched them ride around in there — walk, trot, walk, trot. Fascinating. Like watching a group of prisoners in an exercise yard, except that this bunch seemed to be enjoying themselves.

Three twenty-five. And still no Emily.

I was beginning to get twitchy. Any number of things could have held her up — if she was coming. She might have changed her mind; kids can be mercurial, even serious-minded kids like Emily Hunter. That wouldn't be half as bad as her mother having found out about the phone call and the planned meeting. The quick way Emily had said good-bye yesterday . . . it could've been because her mother walked in on her.

The young equestrians and their instructor kept walking and trotting. And I kept twitching.

Three-thirty.

Three thirty-five.

She wasn't coming. No doubt of it by then, but I stayed put anyway. It was almost four before I called it quits and started the car. The horse smell went away with me, just as I'd known it would.

This being Thursday, Anita Purcell Fine Arts was open for business. Not that they were doing any when I walked in; the place was empty except for a twentyish russet-haired woman sitting at a desk, paging through a catalogue. Either Anita Purcell was very choosy, or fine arts were currently at a premium: the gallery's display stock was on the skimpy side, so much so that the big, white-walled room had an incomplete look, as if Ms. Purcell were in the process of moving in or moving out. Half a dozen large oils and watercolors, the same number of smaller paintings, a couple of marble sculptures, a grouping of pottery and another of porcelain figurines — that was all there was.

The pottery layout was of Sheila Hunter's distinctive blue- and green-glazed, black-design items, and at that there were less than a dozen of them.

The woman hopped to her feet, smiling and eager, as if I were the first potential customer in a long while. She had sea-green eyes, and when I looked into them I felt a little sad. No there there. Like so many individuals you encounter these days, of all types and dispositions. Genetic pod people capable of superficial thought and basic emotions, existing in personal spaces that were dimly lit and mostly empty. The dumbing down of America not only continues, it seems to be approaching epidemic proportions.

She was not Anita Purcell, of course; her name was Gretchen Kiley, she was Ms. Purcell's niece, and she was minding the store while her aunt was away at an auction in Los Angeles. She knew Sheila Hunter, oh, yes, but not very well, and wasn't it a terrible thing about her husband? She guessed Mrs. Hunter and her aunt were friends, and no, she didn't know any of Mrs. Hunter's other friends. Why was I asking? I told her I was conducting a routine investigation on behalf of Jack Hunter's insurance company. Then I took a small flyer because I'd run out of direct questions.

"Does your aunt have any friends, artists, customers named Karen?" I asked.

"Karen?" Blank look. "Uh, why do you want to know that?"

"It pertains to my investigation."

"Oh, it does? Well, I can't think of anyone. I don't know that I should — Oh, wait. Someone named Karen that Mrs. Hunter knows, too, is that what you mean?"

"That's right."

Ms. Kiley gnawed at a well-shaped upper lip. "About a year ago I overheard Aunt Anita and Mrs. Hunter talking about different kinds of art. I mean, I wasn't eavesdropping or anything, I just happened to be here while they were talking. Aunt Anita said she wished she could get some really good stained glass and Mrs. Hunter said she knew someone who made some. A stained-glass artist."

"Someone named Karen."

"I think so. I think that was the name."

"Did she mention a last name?"

Ms. Kiley cudgeled her memory; the effort made her frown and chew on her lip again. "No, I don't think so. Anyway, I can't remember if she did."

"Did she happen to say where Karen lives?"

"Up the coast. That's right, she said 'Karen has a studio up the coast.'"

"Is that all? No town or specific area?"

"No. She stopped right after she said that."

"How do you mean, stopped?"

"All of a sudden. You know, the way you do when somebody interrupts you."

Or the way you do when you're sorry you let something slip. "Did she say anything else about Karen? That she was related to her, for instance?"

"Related? No, I'd remember that."

"Did your aunt seem interested in seeing some of Karen's stained glass?"

"Yes, she did. Mrs. Hunter said Karen was very busy and had outlets for all her work, but she'd tell her and maybe she'd send some things down for Aunt Anita to look at."

"Did Karen ever follow through?"

"Send anything, you mean? I guess not, because we don't have any stained glass, at least I haven't seen any. You'll have to ask my aunt."

"I'll do that," I said. "When will she be back?"

"On Sunday." Ms. Kiley's sunny smile reappeared. "Is there anything I can show you before you leave? We have some really nice pieces of Mrs. Hunter's if you're into pottery."

"No, thanks. I couldn't afford it."

"Well," she said, "do you want me to tell Aunt Anita you stopped by?"

"Not necessary. I'll surprise her."

Ms. Kiley nodded, smiling. She was still standing there, still smiling, when I went out.

The Emerald Hills Country Club was just what you'd expect to find in an affluent enclave like Greenwood. Walled, pillared, gated, manicured, tree-shaded, and overlain with a mossy patina of rustic charm, snooty exclusivity, and very old money. A long drive flanked by poplars led in from a road that ran along the base of the hills. None of the cars in the two-tiered parking area where the drive ended was older than five years or cost much less than I made in a year. Mercedes and BMWs predominated; I spotted a Ferrari, an Aston-Martin, even a Rolls. The scattering of Detroit products seemed almost out of place. Nobody around here paid much attention to the Buy American slogans, it seemed.

The main building was of native stone; I judged its age to be close to the century mark. It had an English manor house look, though some turrets and ramparts and maybe a tower or two were all it would've needed for a castle effect. Behind it to the right I could see outbuildings and some of the greens and fairways, ponds and sand-traps, of the golf course. The grass out there was of such a dazzlingly bright and healthy hue, the groundskeepers might have been giving it daily injections of chlorophyll.

I found a place to park in the designated visitors area on the lower tier. From force of habit I locked the car when I got out, and then smiled wryly to myself when I realized it. Nobody here was going to steal anything out of an old bolt-bucket like mine. If any of the staff or patrons even looked at it twice, it would be to wonder what Emerald Hills was coming to, letting such shoddy merchandise clutter up the grounds.

Well-worn stone steps led up to a wrap-around veranda and a double-door entrance. Inside was a security desk with a discreet placard on it requesting that all members and visitors sign in. A beefy guy in a white polo shirt with *Emerald Hills* stitched over the pocket looked me over and asked with perfect grammar and diction whom I was there to see. He knew I wasn't a member and didn't belong in such a rarified atmosphere, and it showed in his face; employees in places like this can be even bigger elitists than the patrons. Snobs by association. But I was respectable enough in my suit and tie not to be either an anarchist or a tree-hugging rabble-rouser, so when I gave him Trevor Smith's name he nodded and said, "Would you please sign the visitor's book, sir," with the faintest emphasis on the last word. I was tempted to put down somebody else's name — Harry Bridges, for instance, a true rabble-rouser in his day — but I resisted the impulse. It would've been a feeble and petty joke, and he wouldn't have gotten it anyway. Bridges was long dead and so were his longshoremen who'd taken part in the Bloody Thursday labor-management riots in '34, and people nowadays have no sense of history. Except for musty relics like me a stone's throw from being history ourselves.

I walked through the lobby, past entrances to bar and restaurant, a sign that said Ballroom, people in golf outfits and expensive casual wear, older couples in dresses and suits. All the faces were WASP; the only ethnics you were likely to find at Emerald Hills were behind-the-scenes staff members. It was like walking through a small, fancy resort hotel fifty years ago. And I felt as out of place there as a puckered old hound in a kennel full of groomed and pampered show dogs.

74

Another arrow sign pointed the way to the pro shop. It led me outside to the rear, past a crowded terrace overlooking the links and a bank of tennis courts. Nobody was on the courts and not many were driving or putting or riding around in awninged carts; it was the early cocktail hour, the one time of day that was likely to be more important to the country club set than their sport. The pro shop was part of a smaller stone building nearby, in the center of a pair of wings that would house the men's and women's locker rooms.

Inside I found careful displays of clubs and bags and balls, clothing and other items — and a thin middle-aged woman in golf togs who was studying a packaged wristband with a puzzled expression, as if the writing on the package was runic symbols instead of English. Another There-challenged individual, maybe. I waited quietly for a couple of minutes. Nobody else put in an appearance, so I asked the woman if Trevor Smith was around. She barely glanced at me as she said, "He'll be back soon, I'm sure." The wristband package was clearly an object of much greater interest to her than a craggy stranger in an off-the-rack suit.

I wandered over and looked at a rack of

expensive irons and woods. Golf is one of those games that inspire grand passion or grand indifference, and I was firmly in the latter group. I could understand its appeal on an intellectual level, but I never could connect with it emotionally — maybe because I'm not coordinated enough to be any good at the game. The one time I'd let somebody talk me into trying to learn it, it had taken me a week to get over the damage to my ego.

Another couple of minutes, and the little tinkly bell over the door sounded again. But it wasn't Trevor Smith; it was a second middle-aged woman, obviously a friend of the wristband lady because she said, "There you are, Patty." She likewise paid no attention to me, beyond the same kind of cursory glance I'd gotten from the other one.

"I can't decide if I should buy this band or not," Patty said. "It's supposed to be the best, but it gave Ellen Conway a rash. What do you think, Joan?"

"Why don't you ask Trevor?"

"I intend to, if he ever gets back."

"I thought you'd gone up to the Greens Room. You did say you were thirsty."

"I am, God knows. Are the others still there?"

"Waiting for us. Guess who else is still

76

there, staked out at the bar."

"Who? Oh, you mean Dale."

"Drowning herself in gin, as usual. She hasn't drawn a sober breath since the accident. You'd think she'd have come to terms with it by now."

"You'd think so."

"I mean, it was terrible what happened to poor Jack Hunter, but their little affair hadn't been going on very long, and anyway it didn't seem that serious. Did you think it was that serious?"

They might have forgotten about me, if my presence had ever really registered on either of them, or maybe they were the kind of catty gossips who didn't care who happened to overhear them. In any event, they had my full attention now.

"No," Patty said. "Just another of her flings, that's what everyone thought."

"My God, do you suppose she was in love with him?"

"If she was, it was strictly one-sided. Jack would never have left Sheila, no matter how much *she* played around."

"I don't see Dale leaving Frank, either, do you? As much as money and position mean to her."

"No, but if she knows what's good for her, she'll stop all this public lushing and get a grip. Frank's no fool. Word will get back to him, if it hasn't already, and he can add two and two as easily as anyone else. You know him — he won't put up with any sort of obvious nonsense."

"Do you think we should talk to her? Would it do any good?"

"The only person Dale Cooney listens to is herself. If you ask me, the thing to do . . ."

I didn't hear what Patty thought was the thing to do. I didn't much care, for one thing, and for another I was on my way out the door. Trevor Smith could wait. Right now Dale Cooney seemed a potentially better bet.

6

The Greens Room was dominated by a massive native stone fireplace and a wall of sectioned windows that provided a sweeping view of the terrace and tennis courts and golf course. A gas-log fire threw pulsing light over a collection of tables and dark leather booths, about three-quarters of them filled even though it was still a few minutes shy of five o'clock. Most of the ladder-backed stools at the bar were occupied as well. The drinkers there, with one exception, were all men or couples in animated conversation. You didn't need to be much of a detective to figure out that the woman sitting rigidly on the stool near the entrance was in her cups and would answer to the name of Dale Cooney.

I sidled over that way to get a better look at her. Mid-to-late thirties, with the kind of dark, burnished red hair that gleams as

79

black as blood in shadowy bar light. Big-boned body in a cream-colored pants suit. Nice profile, or it would have been if she were sober; at the moment her face and neck had a saggy appearance. Her attention was on the empty martini glass in front of her. Red-nailed fingers tapped a toothpicked olive against the rim, as if she were keeping time to music only she could hear.

A barman in a red jacket came down her way. She raised her head and said, "Charles," not too loudly. "Charles, I believe I'll have one for the road." There was no slur to the words; if anything, her diction was too precise.

"I don't think that's a good idea, Mrs. Cooney."

"You don't? Really?"

"No, ma'am."

"And why not?"

"Six Bombay martinis," he said gently.

"Oh, and such lovely martinis they were. I am a connoisseur of martinis, Charles, did you know that? Well, I am, and yours are the best of all. Almost perfect."

"Yes, ma'am, thank you. But if you don't mind my saying so, I think six is your limit."

"I don't mind at all. Perhaps you're right. Mustn't make a spectacle of myself, must I?"

"No, ma'am."

"Well, then. If you'll bring the check, please."

He went away and came back with it. She studied the strip of paper with a myopic squint, then signed her name at the bottom. Slowly and carefully, the way a child does.

Charles said, "Would you like me to call a taxi for you?"

"I don't believe that will be necessary."

"Are you sure you're able to drive?"

"Quite sure. I haven't exceeded my limit, thanks to your perspicacity. You know what that word means, Charles? Perspicacity?"

"Yes, ma'am. But you don't want to have any trouble getting home."

"I won't have any trouble," she said. "It's only a mile, you know. Exactly one mile from Emerald Hills Country Club to my lovely home. Isn't that interesting?"

"Yes, ma'am. About that taxi . . ."

"Your concern is touching, Charles, it truly is." She maneuvered herself off the stool and onto her feet. No stagger, no unsteadiness — showing the barman that she really was quite all right. She wished him a good evening, turned for the lobby before he could say anything else.

I followed her. She walked as slowly and carefully as she seemed to do everything else, looking straight ahead, her back rigor-mortis stiff. On her dignity, the way some polite, well-bred boozers get when they reach a certain stage of drunkenness. Mustn't make a spectacle of herself.

Outside, the fresh cooling air wobbled her a little, so that she had to steady herself against one of the stone pillars. Down the steps then, using the hand railing, and across the upper level of the parking lot to where a caramel-colored Mercedes 360SL, its top down, was slotted. She was at the driver's door, rummaging in her purse for her keys, when I came up next to her.

"The barman was right, Mrs. Cooney. You'd better not drive."

She blinked, turning her head, and gave me a squinty look. "I don't know you," she said. "Who are you?"

"Somebody who doesn't want to see you hurt or arrested."

"I'm already hurt and I have no intention of being arrested." She squinted again, caught herself doing it this time, and tipped her head back to look at me open-eyed. "You're not a policeman or something, are you?"

"Or something," I said.

"Yes? Well, I'd like to see your badge."

"I don't have a badge."

"Then please go away and leave me alone."

"I can't do that."

"Why can't you? Are you trying to pick me up?"

"No, ma'am."

"Good, because I have a husband and you're as old as he is. I have to drive home to my husband."

"You don't want to do that, Mrs. Cooney."

"No, I don't. But I have to."

"Not after what happened to Jack Hunter, you don't."

Her mouth and her eyes both widened. She made a little murmur in her throat.

"He died because a drunk thought he was sober enough to drive home," I said. "The same thing could happen to you. Lose control of your car, cause the death of an innocent person. Then you'd really have something on your conscience."

She slumped against the Mercedes, gripping the door edge and staring up at me. In a thicker voice she said, "Who *are* you? Did you know Jack?"

"Not personally, no."

"My God," she said with sudden understanding. "My God, you're one of those . . . you're a private detective."

"That's right."

"Frank hired you." Getting that part of it

wrong in a frightened whisper. Her hand was white-knuckled where it clutched the door.

"I'm not working for your husband. I was hired by Jack Hunter's insurance company."

"Insurance?"

"On behalf of his widow — "

"That bitch."

" — and his daughter. Why is Mrs. Hunter a bitch?"

"She made his life miserable."

"How did she do that?"

"Every way. Every damn way."

"Is that what he told you?"

"He didn't have to tell me. I have eyes. Cold-hearted bitch — someday I'll tell her what I think of her. In no uncertain terms."

"Why don't you tell me what you think of her?"

"I just did," she said. "Besides, I have to go home now."

"You're going to have to talk to me, Mrs. Cooney. Not now, but when your head is clear."

"I am not drunk."

I produced one of my business cards, tucked it into her purse. "Will you remember where you got this?"

"Of course I'll remember. I told you, I'm not drunk."

"Then call me. As soon as possible."

"And if I don't?"

"I'll call you. Or stop by and see you."

"Frank," she said. "You wouldn't tell my husband about Jack?"

"I'm not out to do you any harm. All I want are the answers to a few questions about Jack Hunter and his wife. After that, you'll never hear from me again."

"I don't seem to have a choice, do I? All right. But now I have to go home."

"Not just yet. Let me have your keys."

"Oh, no. You can't drive me home, not in my car."

"That isn't my intention. I'll give the keys to the man at the security desk and he can call a taxi for you."

"Oh, no," she said again. A crafty look came into the bleary gray eyes. "Do you want me to scream? I will if you don't go away and let me drive home."

"I don't think you will. You wouldn't want to make a spectacle of yourself."

We locked gazes, but it was not much of a stalemate. The liquor was catching up to her now, making her even more fuzzy-headed and a little shaky on her pins, and she had enough sense to realize it. Her eyes slid away from mine; she fumbled in her purse again, came out with a set of keys, and laid them in my outstretched palm almost gently. On her dignity again.

I said, "Do you want to wait inside?"

"No, thank you. I'll sit here in the car."

She opened the door, put herself under the wheel with great care, and sat looking straight ahead, hands clasped in her lap, spine rigid.

"Tell them to hurry," she said. "I really need to get home before Frank does."

That was part of the reason, I thought as I left her, but not all of it. The sooner she got home, the sooner she could have another drink.

Joan and Patty were gone when I returned to the pro shop. The lone occupant now, separating the day's receipts into piles of cash and chits, was a muscular, sun-browned guy dressed in tan chamois slacks and an Emerald Hills polo shirt. He was about forty, with one of those handsome chiseled profiles that were assurances of box-office success among male film stars a generation ago. A thick mat of curly hair the color of pale ale topped him off to masculine perfection. Women like Joan and Patty would want to take lessons from him, all right, off the golf course as well as on it. He was the type of physical specimen who could have a different bed partner every night of the year if he wanted it that way. The question was whether or not he was that type.

He had a polite smile for me as I came up to the counter. The neutral variety, without any of the disdain of the guy on the security desk. Point in his favor.

"Help you, sir?"

"You can if you're Trevor Smith."

"Guilty. Don't believe I've seen you here before." Friendly, cheerful, no signs of either arrogance or conceit. Another point in his favor.

"I've never been here before," I said. When he'd had a look at the card I handed him, I added, "I represent Intercoastal Insurance — "

That was as far as I got. His smile vanished, his face set hard and tight, and he said with a kind of simmering anger, "So you're the one. Who told you to come sucking around here?"

"Could be the same person who told you about me."

"No way. Whoever it was, I don't care what they said. Sheila Hunter and I are friends, that's all."

"Then maybe you have some idea why she's so dead set against capitalizing on her husband's insurance policy."

"If I did, I wouldn't tell you. It's her business."

"And her daughter's."

"Not yours or the insurance company's, that's the point. Why don't you leave her alone? Her husband's been dead less than two weeks, for Christ's sake."

"I'm sorry about her loss," I said. "But it doesn't explain why she's so afraid."

"Afraid? What're you talking about?"

"I think you know what I'm talking about, Mr. Smith. If you've seen her lately you couldn't help but know."

He knew, all right, and it was bothering him; I could see it in his eyes. More between Sheila Hunter and him than a casual friendship, a casual affair?

"She doesn't want her past investigated," I said. "Why? What's she afraid I'll find out?"

"That's bull," Smith said. "You can't make me believe she's hiding anything about her past."

"I won't try. But I believe she is. She's been living a lie the past ten years, she and her husband both."

"What does that mean, a lie?"

"She ever say anything to you about her life before they came to Greenwood? Where they lived, what they did?"

No answer. But his silence was eloquent.

"Does the word crazybone mean anything to you?"

"Crazy — Now what the hell?"

"It means something to her, something bad. Ask her about it. Ask her about her past."

"Why should I? Listen — "

"I might be able to help her. I already know some of the truth and if I keep digging I'll find out the rest. It's going to come out one way or another."

He leaned forward across the counter so that his face was close to mine. I let him do it without giving ground. "Blackmail?" he said. "Is that your damn game?"

"No, and don't use that word to me again. I don't like it."

"I don't like you or what you're doing to Sheila."

"Your prerogative. But all I'm trying to do, all I'm going to do, is my job. And all I want out of it is the fee I'm being paid by Intercoastal Insurance. The truth is my game, Smith. The only other thing I'm interested in is Emily Hunter's welfare."

"Now you're saying Sheila is an unfit mother, is that it?"

"No. I'm saying whatever she's hiding, whatever she and her husband were mixed up in before they came to Greenwood, may

89

be putting the child's future in jeopardy. I don't want to see that happen. Do you?"

Smith's eyes held on mine a few seconds longer. Then the anger went out of him and he backed off. Worry and dismay were what I was looking at then.

"She won't talk to me," he said. "I've tried . . . she just walls herself off."

"It might be different when you tell her what I've told you."

"I don't know. If it's bad enough, the thing she's so scared of . . ."

"It may not be as bad as she thinks it is. Even if it's a police matter, it may not be."

A muscle jumped on Smith's cheek; it pulled one side of his mouth up in a puckery rictus. "Christ," he said.

"Will you try to get her to talk to me?"

"I don't know . . ."

"At her house, some public place, whatever. You can be there, too, if she wants it that way."

Long pause. Then, "All right, I'll try. But you better be on the level about helping her. If you're not — "

"I can give you a dozen references."

His eyes probed mine, for ten seconds or so this time. Then he shook his head: a gesture of silent acceptance.

"My home and office numbers are on the

card," I said. "Any time, day or night."

"All right." And then, almost plaintively, "She really is scared. Like a kid in the dark."

"I know."

"I can't stand to see her like that. It makes me — "

He broke off and swung away, quickly, as if there was something in his face he didn't want me to see. I had a pretty good idea what it was. Maybe he'd been a trophy collector in the past, what Tamara would call an "ass bandit," and maybe he wasn't that type at all, but in any event there was more to Trevor Smith than just a hunk's body and a pretty face.

He was in love with Sheila Hunter. About as deeply in love as a man can be with a woman.

Thursday evening. No call from Emily Hunter, or Sheila Hunter, or Trevor Smith, or Dale Cooney.

Friday morning. Nothing from any of them.

Friday afternoon. Nothing.

All the silence worried me. Not so much Mrs. Cooney's; boozers are unpredictable drunk or sober, and she figured to have the least amount of information for me. But why hadn't Emily kept our appointment and

91

why hadn't she gotten in touch again? And had I scared her mother even more by taking the risk of confiding in Smith? For all I knew, whatever had caused the Hunters to change their identity ten years ago was a felony of major proportions, and in that case aiming Smith at her might've been the same as aiming a loaded gun. The last thing I wanted was to panic her, but I could have done just that. What would she do then? And how would it affect her daughter?

At four o'clock, just before I left the office to meet Kerry at Bates and Carpenter, I called the Emerald Hills Country Club and asked for the pro shop. The operator said it was closed today. No, Trevor Smith wasn't at the club; he had called in ill. And no, she would not give me his home number, no matter what kind of emergency I said it was. I had Tamara look him up in the San Mateo and Santa Clara county phone directories while I tried the Hunters' number. No answer there. And no listing for Trevor Smith.

"Goddamn it!" I said.

Tamara said, "Easy, boss. Remember what you always tell me about jumping to conclusions?"

"Yeah." But suppose the conclusion I was jumping to was the right one? Suppose I'd screwed up the Hunter situation big time?

7

If there is one thing I'm not, it's a party animal.

I do not deal well with large gatherings in enclosed spaces. Give me a job to do and a one-on-one or even a small-group circumstance and I relate well enough; I'm able to think on my feet and hold my own in a conversation. But plunk me down in the midst of a cocktail party where social interaction with strangers is required, and I curl up inside like a worm in a bottle. I'm no good at small talk. And not much of a drinker; too much alcohol in a party atmosphere has the opposite effect on me than it does on most people, making me withdraw even more. The bigger the crowd, the worse I feel. Crush of bodies, too-loud voices, the constant strain . . . I start out edgy and if I'm trapped long enough I tend to become claustrophobic. Not enough space or air to breathe.

So I knew going in to the party at Bates and Carpenter that it would be a two-hour ordeal. And the agitated mood I was in would only make it worse. But I'd promised Kerry, and if I got through the cocktail party, the dinner afterward would be a piece of cake by comparison. So on the way over to the ad agency I played a little self-psyching game, blocking out the Hunter case and reminding myself that this evening was a small price to pay for all that Kerry had done for me and promising myself rewards for being a good boy and making the best of what, after all, was only a couple of hours out of the rest of my life. The trick seemed to work at first; I was calmly resigned and wearing a half-hearty facade when I met Kerry in her office. She seemed relieved, as if she'd expected me to come in looking like a man attending his own funeral. She even commented on my "upbeat mood" as we went upstairs — Bates and Carpenter had two floors in an old building on lower Geary downtown — to the big conference room where the party was being held.

The psych job, though, began to develop cracks once we arrived. Twenty-five or so people were already there, most of them clustered around a full-service bar and a table of hors d'oeuvres at one end, chattering and laughing noisily. On a quick scan I saw several of Kerry's co-workers, Jim Carpenter prominent among them, naturally, and two other faces I recognized: Kerry's crazy friend Paula Hanley, who owned an interior design company and was a B&C client, and her tubby chiropractor husband, Andrew. Terrific. Paula was a magnet for every screwball fad that came along, had a passion for "improving" other people's lives through proselytism, and managed to set my teeth on edge in the best of circumstances. In a party atmosphere she might well be lethal.

Carpenter came over first, towing his latest conquest, a sloe-eyed blonde half his age. Handsome bastard, with his silver mane and dark (probably dyed) mustache. He shook my hand and asked how I was in his vaguely condescending fashion. He'd had a thing for Kerry once and his attitude toward her was still irritatingly proprietary; he kissed her — on the mouth, no less — as if he hadn't seen her in weeks and let his hand linger on her arm. I stood by and watched this and smiled and thought about what his neck would feel like in a circle of my fingers.

Then came Mr. and Mrs. Anthony DiGrazia of DiGrazia's Old-Fashioned Italian Sausages. They were both in their mid-sixties, both short and very round and very red-faced; the only physical difference between them, in fact, seemed to be that he was bald and she had a pile of expensively coiffed blue hair. Their personalities, however, were total opposites, like a photograph and its negative. He was smiling, outgoing, voluable, and prone to punctuating his words with hand and arm gestures in the classic Italian manner. She was silent, stiff, and wore an expression that said her shoes pinched her feet, her girdle was too tight, her stomach was upset, and she didn't approve of occasions like this one or much of anything except maybe the diamonds and rubies on her fingers and at her throat. Dragon lady. And ruler of the DiGrazia roost, I had no doubt.

Mr. DiGrazia pumped my hand in an iron grip and asked in Italian after my health. I said, *"Benissimo. Come sano uno cavallino."* He liked that; he laughed and slapped me on the back.

"So, paisan," he said, "you eat plenty of sausage and salami, eh?"

"Sure. Plenty."

"*My* sausage and salami?"

"I wouldn't eat any other kind, Mr. DiGrazia," I lied again.

"Tony. I'm Tony, you're Phil." For some

reason he'd got it into his head that my first name was Phil and no attempt by Kerry or me or anybody else during the evening convinced him otherwise. "New world elegance, old world taste. What you think, Phil?"

"About what?"

"New world elegance, old world taste."

He was looking at me expectantly. I said, "I'm not sure I — "

"What, Kerry, you don't talk to your husband? Tell him what good ideas you got?"

"I only came up with the slogan today," she said, and nudged my arm. "DiGrazia's Old-Fashioned Italian Sausages. New world elegance, old world taste."

"Oh," I said. "Slogan."

"You like it, huh, Phil?"

"I like it."

"I like it, too. You like it, Roseanna?"

"No," Mrs. DiGrazia said.

This nonplussed Kerry. "Well, you know, it's only a preliminary working — "

"Sure, sure," Tony said. "Kerry's good, she's the best, I'm not worried." He clapped me on the back again. "Listen, Phil, they got a whole table of my sausage and salami over there, plenty of wine, anything else you want to drink. You and me, we go over and eat some sausage, drink some wine, let the wives get better acquainted."

We went and he ordered two glasses of Chianti without consulting me and then loaded up a couple of plates. He said, "Salute," and clinked his glass against mine, after which he tossed off half his wine at a gulp. "So, Phil, tell me about the detective business."

"There's not much to tell. It's a job like any other — "

"Nah, come on. Pretty exciting, eh? I see your name in the papers sometimes, you don't get your name in the papers if you got a job like any other job."

"Well, once in a while there's some excitement. Mostly, though — "

"You meet plenty good-looking women, eh?"

"Well . . ."

"Sexy young blondes with big tits. Few of those, eh?"

"Well . . ."

He leaned close to me; his eyes were very bright. "How many times you screw one on your desk?"

"What? Uh, I've never — "

"Big tits, little tits, you never screwed one in your office? Desk, floor, how about a couch you got in there?"

"No. Look, Tony — "

"I always wanted to do that," he said

98

wistfully. He finished his wine in another swallow. "Screw a sexy young blonde, bada boom, bada bing, right there in my office. Once I had a chance, this secretary I had, but she was too old, too fat, fatter than Roseanna. Gotta be worth it, you take a risk like that. You know what I mean, Phil?"

"Yeah, I know what you mean."

"You ever screw somebody in your office, you make sure it's worth it, make sure she's some sexy young blonde with big tits. And don't let Kerry find out. I like Kerry, I don't want to see her unhappy."

Jim Carpenter saved me from any more of this by bringing up somebody he wanted DiGrazia to meet. I wandered back to where Kerry had extricated herself from the dragon lady. She said, "You seem to be getting along pretty well with Tony. He's a sweet old guy, isn't he?"

This was not the time or the place to tell her about Tony's favorite fantasy. I said, "That's one way to describe him," and let it go at that.

Kerry dragged me around and introduced me to some people. That wasn't so bad because she was right there beside me, but the room was filling up, spilling over into the smaller one adjacent, the noise level was up into the high-decibel range, and it was inevitable the shifting tide of bodies would pull us apart and I'd be on my own. The guy who wrote that no man is an island must never have been lost in the stormy sea of an overblown cocktail party.

The last thing Kerry said to me before we got separated was, "You'll be fine. Just go ahead and mingle." Right. I was mingling by myself in a corner, hanging on to a fresh glass of red wine with both hands, when a woman I'd never seen before came sidling up. Sexy young blonde with a well-developed chest — if DiGrazia saw her, he'd probably try to hire her on the spot.

"Hello," she said.

"Hello," I said.

"Are you anybody?" she asked.

". . . I'm sorry?"

"Anybody. You know, in the advertising business."

"I'm not in the advertising business."

"Oh. Well, are you anybody in any other business?"

"I don't know what you mean by anybody."

"You know, important. Are you important?"

"Only to myself and my wife, and then not all the time."

"Does that mean no?"

"Yes. I mean, no."

"Well, which is it?"

"No," I said.

"I thought so," she said, and walked away.

I was standing there wondering what had just happened when another woman's voice said, "There you are." Talking to me — and I wished she wasn't. Paula Hanley, with Andrew in tow.

"We've been looking all over for you," she said in her shrill, breathless voice. "Haven't we, Andrew?"

"Oh, sure," Andrew said.

"Isn't this a fun party?"

"I can think of better words for it," I said.

As usual Paula was a vision — the kind an acidhead might have on a bad trip. Lemon-yellow hair, pumpkin-colored lipstick, a sea-green outfit topped off by three or four scarves in violent shades of purple and orange. One of the most expensive interior designers in the city and she looked like the survivor of a paint factory explosion. Go figure.

"It's been months since we've seen you," she said. "Hasn't it been months, Andrew?"

"Months," Andrew agreed. He took a sip from a very large glass of what I guessed was gin. That and the mixture of boredom and annoyance in his expression said he didn't want to be here any more than I did.

"How're things on the god and goddess front?" I asked Paula. It was the only conversational gambit I could come up with.

"The what?"

"New Age tantra. *The Holy Sexual Communion.*" That had been her grand passion the last time I'd seen her — a sexual enhancement fad based on a 1500-year-old tradition that involved chanting, massages with scented oil, beating on elkskin drums, and providing private parts with names like Wand of Light and Valley of Bliss.

"Oh," Paula said, "we're not into that anymore."

Big surprise; she changed fads as often as she changed underwear. "Didn't work out, huh?"

"Oh, no, it was a wonderful few months. Spiritual love in which orgasm is truly nonessential. Wasn't it wonderful, Andrew?"

Andrew took another large sip from his large glass. "One of the crowning experiences of my life," he said.

She gave him a look, decided he wasn't being sarcastic, and said to me, "We've progressed into other areas of intimacy, with even greater satisfaction. Of course I can't discuss them in an atmosphere like this, but if you and Kerry are interested . . ."

"No," I said quickly. "We're just fine in the intimacy department. Everything working the way it should."

Andrew snickered.

Paula asked me, "Have you tried acupuncture?"

"What, as a sexual aid?"

"No, no. As a method of healing."

"I don't like needles."

"I don't, either. You hardly feel the ones they use. And they're the disposable ones, of course, so you don't have to worry about disease."

"I'll take your word for it."

"Acupuncture is marvelous," Paula said, in the ecstatic tone she reserves for brand-new fads and follies. "It cures all kinds of ailments — arthritis, bursitis, insomnia, allergies — "

"It doesn't *cure* anything," Andrew said. "It's quack medicine."

She turned on him. "How can you say that?"

"I can say it because it's true. It's in the same class with massage, herbal treatments, and spiritual healing."

"Alternative therapies, every one," Paula said with acid sweetness. "Isn't chiropractic considered alternative therapy?"

Red splotches appeared on Andrew's puffy cheeks. "Just because the goddamn

103

A.M.A. refuses to recognize the benefits of chiropractic medicine — "

"*Or* the benefits of acupuncture." She swiveled my way again. "It really does work. For a while I had serious digestive problems, and they vanished, I mean completely vanished, after only three sessions with Dr. Dong. And what he did for my sciatica — "

"Dr. Dong. My God!"

"Andrew, the man can't help the name he was born with. Besides, Dong is a perfectly common Chinese name — "

"And he's a perfectly common Chinese quack."

"He is not a quack! He has been in business twenty-five years, he's a graduate of the Shanghai Chinese Medical School and diplomate of the National Board of Acupuncture Orthopedics — "

"Diplomate. What the hell is a diplomate?"

"It's the same thing as a diplomat, isn't it? Well, never mind. Dr. Dong has all sorts of degrees and testimonials — "

"Bought and paid for, no doubt."

" — from satisfied patients like myself. He cured my digestive problems and he did wonders for my sciatica. *You* couldn't do anything about my sciatica, could you?"

"I could have if you'd let me use proper

chiropractic techniques. But no, you screamed every time I tried to — "

"You were *hurting* me. The pain doubled every time you poked and twisted — "

"*You're* a double pain sometimes," Andrew muttered. "And not in my sciatica."

She skewered him with the famous Hanley glare. "How dare you talk to me like that in public. You're drunk, aren't you? Gin on an empty stomach. How many times have I told you — "

"Let me count the number."

"I'm warning you, Andrew . . ."

I edged away from them — they didn't even notice — and joined the party flow. Anything was better than listening to the Hanleys imitate that old radio couple, the Bickersons.

I was now a floating island, but nobody paid any attention to me. I looked around for another corner in which to drop anchor, spotted one, and was on my way when two things gave me pause. Both were part of the same individual, a skinny, ascetic type in tinted glasses and a polka-dot bowtie. The bowtie was one of the things that stopped me; it made him even more of a dinosaur than me. The other was his voice, which he was using loudly to an audience of two older women.

"The advertising racket," he was declaiming, "is a prime example of what's wrong with modern society. Strip away the fancy veneer and what have you got except hype and bullshit? Same bottom line for the federal government, state and local governments, big business, the media, the entertainment industry, pretty much anything you can name. Hype and bullshit, that's what the country runs on nowadays. We're bombarded by it, it shapes everything we see and hear and do. There's no truth anymore, no sincerity, humility, honesty. All there is is exaggeration, distortion, out and out lies. Hype, hype, hype, crap, crap, crap. You remember the Peter Finch character in *Network*? Saying he was sick and tired of all the bullshit? Well, that's exactly what I'm saying. I'm sick and tired of all the deceiving, loudmouth, self-aggrandizing bullshit. I'm mad as hell and I'm not going to take it anymore. Every chance I get I'm going to stand up and shout it like it is. You remember the John Goodman character in *The Big Lebowski*? How he kept telling the Steve Buscemi character, 'Shut the fuck up, Donnie,' every time he opened his stupid yap? Well, every time I hear somebody shovel up another load of hype and bullshit I'm going to stand up and say — "

"Shut the fuck up, Harlan," one of the women said.

"We're sick and tired of all the bullshit," the other woman said. "We're mad as hell and we're not going to take it anymore."

The two of them left Bowtie standing there with his mouth open. It was one of those pristine little moments, made all the more satisfying by the fact that he seemed to have no idea whatsoever of how thoroughly he'd been squelched.

I took up residence in the new corner, feeling slightly better than I had before Harlan got his. No one bothered me at first, which allowed me to pretend I was a hidden observer, like a spy camera in a potted plant. I spotted Kerry twice; she tried to make her way over to me and was accosted and side-tracked both times. Then Anthony DiGrazia found me and spoiled my peaceful illusion. He bent my ear about the sausage business, then launched into a diatribe on capital punishment. He was in favor of it; in fact, he seemed to believe that all felons, including pickpockets and hubcap thieves, ought to be subjected to lethal injection for their transgressions.

His ten-minute harangue was winding down when we were suddenly confronted by an intense young woman — not, thank God, a sexy blonde but a too-thin individual with brown hair that looked as if it had been cut with a weed-whacker. She fixed each of us with a glazed eye and said, "Which one of you is Anthony DiGrazia?"

"That's me, little lady. You like my party?"

"No," she said.

"No?"

"No. I just want you to know I think it's disgusting."

"What, my party?"

"That stuff you make. That sausage."

"My sausage is disgusting?"

"Absolutely." She tapped his clavicle with a bony forefinger. "Made out of dead animals. Poor defenseless pigs and cows and goats."

"Goats? Hey, we don't use — "

"Blood, ground-up bones, strands of hair — "

"What? In my sausage? *Hair?*"

" — and all sorts of disgusting organs. Fat, cholesterol, sodium, malonaldehyde, aflaxtons . . . don't you know you're giving people heart attacks and cancer?"

"*Cacchio!* Heart attacks, cancer? Listen, lady, all I give people is good meat, the best meat. My sausage is so pure you can feed it to a baby."

"What a horrible thing to say. Isn't it bad

enough you feed your poison to adults? A feast of bacteria! Germ warfare!"

"By God, we don't allow no germs in my factory — "

"Why don't you manufacture food that's healthy and nutritious? Soybeans, tofu — "

"Gaah!" DiGrazia said.

"Soybeans and tofu are healthy foods."

"You say food, I say crap."

"You ought to be ashamed of yourself."

"Hah. You, you're for shame, you crazy food nazi."

"Better a food nazi than a mass murderer," the woman said, and made it her exit line.

DiGrazia watched her stalk off into the throng. *"Pazzo,"* he said, tapping his temple. "All those vegetarian animal rights food nazis, crazy in the head. Germs, heart attacks, cancer — you know how many times I heard crap like that, Phil? Ten thousand times, I heard it once. It don't even bother me much anymore. Life's too short, you got to take the bad with the good. So what'd you think of her ass, eh?"

The non sequitur made me blink. "What?"

"Her ass. Not bad for a skinny *cogliona*. Not much in the tit department, but a nice ass and plenty of fire. Fire in the mouth, fire

109

in the ass — you know what I mean, Phil?"

"Is that all you ever think about?"

The words were out before I could bite them back, but he didn't seem to notice my annoyance. Or to be offended by it if he did. "Sure," he said. "Roseanna, she says I got sausage on the brain. 'That's all you ever think about,' she says, 'your sausage.' She don't know how right she is, eh? I see a good-looking woman, nice ass, plenty of fire, that's just what I'm thinking about. DiGrazia's sausage." He laughed and winked. "I think I go find that food nazi, talk to her some more. Don't hurt to try, eh, Phil? You never know. *Cogliona* like that, hates you one minute, you talk to her right and the next minute maybe she changes her mind. Bada boom, bada bing, maybe she ends up sampling my sausage after all."

He winked again and waddled off, leaving me mercifully alone and wishing I were in Fresno or even wandering in the middle of Death Valley. I moved over against the nearest wall and looked at my watch, with hope at first and then in disbelief and dull dread.

It was only twenty til six. I'd been here less than forty-five minutes.

And the party swirled on.

And on.

And on . . .

110

8

In the morning I woke up with a headache, a fuzzy taste in my mouth, a sour stomach, and enough gas to power a modern version of the *Hindenburg*. Hangover supreme, courtesy of Anthony DiGrazia. Not so much red wine- or party-induced as the product of a heaping plateful of fried peppers, garlic, and DiGrazia's Old-Fashioned Italian Sausage. He'd insisted we have dinner at a North Beach restaurant owned by a friend of his, and then insisted we all have the chef's house special. With garlic bread, naturally, and three or maybe six bottles of vintage Rubbino Chianti. In addition to having a heart full of unrequited lust and a head full of reactionary ideas on crime and punishment, the man was of the same breed, different genus, as the intense young woman with the weed-whacked hair — a food nazi.

Kerry stirred beside me. I looked over at

her, and she muttered a good morning without making eye contact. "You feel as bad as
I do?" I asked her.

"Worse. And don't you dare say you're
glad."

"I want a divorce."

"What?"

"I thought you should know what the
words sound like. You'll hear them again if
you ever try talking me into another evening
like the last one."

"I wouldn't try to talk myself into another
evening like the last one."

I got up, drank an Alka-Seltzer, brushed
my teeth, took a shower, swallowed another
Alka-Seltzer, brushed my teeth again, and
put clothes on. When I came back into the
bedroom, Kerry was still lying in bed looking miserable.

"Rise and shine," I said. "Lunch with
Cybil at noon."

"Oh, Lord, that's right."

"Maybe she'll fix us something with
Italian sausage."

Kerry groaned and pulled the covers over
her head.

After I made coffee I checked the answering machine again. There hadn't been a
message from anybody in Greenwood last
night and none had magically appeared this

morning. I called the office and accessed the machine there. No message. An e-mail, maybe? My business cards now had the office e-mail address, the result of Tamara's urging. I thought about calling her, decided it was too early on a Saturday morning, and that in my condition I couldn't stand being yelled at for interrupting the rising of Mr. Sun, and waited for Kerry to get up. She keeps a pc in her study and she had the good sense not to chide me, as she sometimes does, about being too stubborn to learn even rudimentary computer skills. She accessed the office e-mail for me. And that was a bust, too.

One more day, I thought bleakly. If I don't hear from somebody by this time tomorrow, I'll go down there and shake a few trees until something falls out.

Cybil said, "You smell like garlic and stale wine. Both of you."

"Oh, God," Kerry said, "and I gargled three times and brushed my teeth twice this morning."

"It gets into the pores, dear."

"You have any Alka-Seltzer?" I asked her.

"No. Out carousing last night, were you?"

"Carousing isn't the word for it."

"A business dinner that didn't turn out

well," Kerry explained briefly. "Is that chicken pot pie I smell?"

"It is. Very soothing to an alcohol-ravaged stomach."

"Hah," I said. "As if you didn't take a drink yourself now and then."

"Always in moderation."

"Sure, moderation. I know all about those drunken orgies you and Russ Dancer and your other pulp-writer pals used to indulge in."

"Scurrilous lies. I have never been to an orgy in my life."

"That you can remember."

"Oh, I remember all of my escapades."

"And there've been some doozies, I'll bet."

"You'll never know."

Cybil wasn't ready yet to talk about Archie Todd; she bustled around her tiny kitchen getting lunch ready, while Kerry and I took up space in the living room. The bungalow was a small two-bedroom, one half of a duplex with a shared back patio; she used the second bedroom as her office. This and Redwood Village's other duplex cottages were surrounded by well-tended lawns and flower beds and shaded by redwoods. Among other amenities on the five acres were rec room, dining hall, swimming pool, and putting green. Nice, quiet little enclave in the nice, quiet little town of Larkspur. And Cybil had thrived in it. When Kerry's father, Ivan, died a couple of years back, and Cybil sold their L.A. house and moved in with Kerry, she had been lost and dying by degrees herself. The move to Redwood Village had literally saved her life. Not only had it allowed her to regain her independence, it had given her back her zest for living and her desire to write fiction.

A copy of her recently published first novel, *Dead Eye*, was prominently displayed on the end table next to where I was sitting. Her brag copy, she called it. I'd already read the book, but I picked up the copy and glanced through it again. A remarkably smooth and polished period piece, set in L.A. during the Communist witch hunts of the early 1950s. It was as though there had been no more of a gap than a few months between Samuel Leatherman's last pulp-magazine adventure, published in those same early fifties, and his first full-length case. She was something, Cybil was. No woman who had produced both a tough-as-nails hero like Leatherman and a daughter like Kerry, and put up with a contentious anal retentive like Ivan Wade for fifty years, could be anything but special.

She was troubled now, though. The sharp wit and cheerful demeanor were like the clothes she'd donned for the occasion: dress-up facade. There were gloomy depths in her tawny eyes. Kerry noticed it, too; I could tell by the concerned look she gave me when Cybil left us alone.

Over lunch the talk was superficial dead-air filler. I kept waiting for Cybil to bring up Archie Todd's name and it kept not happening. Kerry toed me under the table once and I toed her back and went on eating. The pot pie was very good. Soothing, too, as Cybil had said. And I deal better with family and professional matters on a full stomach.

Kerry delivered another not-so-gentle nudge as I finished my second helping. Okay, time for me to prime the pump. I said to Cybil, "Kerry tells me Captain Archie passed away recently. I was sorry to hear it."

"Passed away," she said. "Such a silly euphemism."

"What would you prefer? Croaked?"

That earned me another poke, but Cybil said, "Rubbed out would do better. It's old-fashioned but accurate."

"You're not saying he was murdered?"

"No, I'm not, because I have no proof he was. But it's what I suspect."

"You're serious," I said.

"Of course I'm serious. Would I make a joke about a thing like that?"

"What makes you suspect foul play?"

She pressed her lips together and stared out through the window. From where she was sitting she could look across tree-shadowed lawn and the street out front to where other cottages were spaced at intervals. Looking at the one Captain Archie had occupied, maybe.

"Cybil, how did he die?"

"Congestive heart failure," she said. "He died in his bed sometime during the night."

"Well, if that's the case, it's the best way any of us can go."

"It would be if that was all there was to it. Dr. Lengel thinks so, because Archie had CHF disease — that's a reduction in the ability of the heart to pump blood. CHF patients often die from ventricular fibrillation, a sudden heart attack."

"Lengel's the resident physician here?" Redwood Village had a small clinic with a doctor and nurse on call twenty-four hours.

"Yes. He signed the death certificate."

"So if Captain Archie had a bad heart and there's no question of how he died . . . ?"

"Congestive heart failure can be induced by an overdose of digitoxin, the medication he was taking to regulate his heartbeat. His

117

maintainence dose was 0.05 milligrams per day. His prescription — from his own physician, Dr. Johannsen — was for pills of exactly that dosage, to be taken one every evening at bedtime. But the night he died he was given or forced to swallow a larger dosage."

"How can you know that?"

"Well, to begin with, I'm the one who found him."

Kerry blinked at her. "How did you — "

"We were friends, good friends. Archie had been depressed and I went over early that morning to see if I could cheer him up."

"How did you get in? Was his door unlocked?"

"I have a key. And it's none of your business why."

"What about this digitoxin overdose?" I asked.

"Archie's pills, the prescribed 0.05 dosage, were orange. When I went back later, after his body was taken away, I found a pink pill that must have been dropped and accidentally kicked under the bed. I had a feeling something was amiss and the pink pill confirmed it."

"The pink pill did."

"That's right. Pink is the color of a 0.10 dosage, twice what Archie was permitted to take each day."

"Are you sure it was digitoxin?"

"Positive. Of that and of the dosage. I showed the pink pill to my own doctor."

"Maybe it was from an old prescription of Archie's. Maybe it'd been under the bed a long time."

"Archie never took a dosage larger than 0.05," Cybil said. "He told me so himself. And there was plenty of dust under his bed but none on the pill."

"He didn't get the larger dosage from Dr. Lengel, by any chance?"

"No. And there were no other pink digitoxin pills in his unit. I know because I looked."

"And that's why you think he was murdered, the one pink pill you found?"

"Essentially, yes."

"That's pretty thin evidence, Cybil."

"Don't you think I know that?"

"You haven't talked to the local police, have you?"

She gave me an up-from-under look, the prototype of the one Kerry used on me from time to time. "Of course not."

"Told anyone else of your suspicion? Dr. Lengel? Dr. Johannsen? The Captain's attorney?"

"No. An autopsy would corroborate the overdose, I'm sure, but Dr. Lengel saw no reason to request one and no one else will either without evidence of foul play. Besides, I don't care to be considered a foolish, fanciful old lady by anyone including my daughter and son-in-law."

"Did I say you were foolish and fanciful?"

"It's what you're thinking."

"No, it isn't," I said. "I don't doubt your good sense and neither does Kerry. I'm just trying to understand why you're so sure it was murder. Why not suicide? You said Captain Archie was depressed and his health was poor. He could've gotten the larger dose of digitoxin himself, some way — "

"He did not commit suicide," Cybil said.

"How can you be so sure?"

"Archie Todd was a devout Catholic. He attended Mass regularly every Sunday."

"Oh," I said.

Kerry said, "Why exactly was he depressed?"

"I don't know. He wouldn't talk about it. But it was more than just general melancholy — he was angry about something. Very angry the day before his death."

"You've no idea why?"

"The only thing he ever said to me was that he'd made a terrible mistake, he should never have trusted the bastards. His exact words."

120

"Friends or business associates who deceived him in some way," I said. "Or old enemies come back into his life."

"I can't imagine who would want to do him any kind of harm. Archie Todd was a gentle, easygoing man. He got along with everyone."

"Profit is the obvious motive. How large is his estate?"

"I can't tell you exactly. I would guess six figures, mostly in stocks and mutual funds."

"Then he must've had a broker or investment counselor."

"Dunbar Asset Management."

One of San Francisco's largest financial management outfits; even I had heard of them. "Who's the executor of his estate?"

"Evan Patterson, Archie's attorney."

"Local?"

"Yes. He has an office on Magnolia Avenue."

"And who inherits? Captain Archie had no living relatives, did he?"

"Only one. A niece in Connecticut. But he hadn't seen her in twenty-five or thirty years and he told me once he'd left her out of his will. His entire estate goes to the San Francisco Maritime Museum, along with his collection of ferryboating memorabilia. He loved ferries, you know, and he was an expert on their history and lore. The bequest was to establish a permanent museum exhibit in his name."

"Well, there goes the only motive that makes sense."

"Unless someone was after his collection," Kerry said. "Is that possible, Cybil? If it's valuable enough — "

"Its value is mainly historical. I suppose another collector might be willing to pay dearly for it, but the bulk of the collection is already in storage at the museum. Archie let them have it four years ago, when he moved over here from the city, as a stipulation of his bequest."

I said, "Okay. So what all this boils down to is, you want me to conduct an investigation based on not much more than a hunch and a pink pill. I don't see what I can — "

"Did I say I wanted you to conduct an investigation?"

"That's why you asked us to lunch, isn't it?"

"Smart guy. All right, then. I'll pay your standard fee."

"You will like hell. I won't take money from you."

"You take money from strangers."

"That's different. You're family."

"Crap," Cybil said. "Samuel Leatherman would take it in a New York minute."

"I'm not Samuel Leatherman."

"And a good thing, too. If I were writing stories about you I'd still be an unpublished writer."

"Cybil," I said with a tight grip on my patience. "Cybil, I'm only trying to tell you that I doubt there's much I can do without something more to work with."

"So you won't even try."

Kerry said, "Of course he'll try. Won't you, dear?"

I said, "Ow," because she'd poked me again. Hard.

"Let him alone, Kerry. If he thinks I'm a silly old lady pursuing a fantasy, well, I can't really blame him. After all, he's more experienced in these matters . . ."

"Will you knock off that silly old lady stuff? You're as smart and wily as they come and you know it. If you're convinced that Captain Archie was murdered I'm not going to argue with you, I'll give you the benefit of the doubt."

"Does that mean you'll look into it?"

"Yes, okay, I'll look into it. As a favor. No money — don't bring up the subject of money again. Monday morning I'll check with Evan Patterson — "

"Why wait until Monday? Why not start now?"

"Lawyers don't work on Saturday, you know that."

"I don't mean Evan Patterson. I mean you could go over to Archie's unit and have a look through his things."

"It's all still there?"

"It is. Patterson hasn't been able to locate the niece, and Archie's rent is paid through the end of the month."

"Uh-huh. Don't tell me you haven't been over there snooping around — more than once, I'll bet. If you didn't find anything, there's nothing there to find."

"I'm not a detective," she said. "You are."

"You write detective stories — you know what to look for and where to look as well as I do."

"Balls. The difference is that you're a professional snoop and I'm only an amateur. Will you go and look?"

"It'd be trespassing. I don't have any right to enter and search a premises without permission."

She rolled her eyes. "You have *my* permission. I was his friend, his close friend, and he entrusted me with a key. I'll take full responsibility."

"Can I at least have some dessert first?"

Kerry said, "When you come back."

Cybil said, "I'll get the key."

Judging from the furnishings in his one-bedroom duplex, Captain Archie had lived something of a Spartan existence. The living room contained an old, deep, cracked-leather armchair, a small portable TV on a stand, a rickety secretary desk that looked as if it might have had nautical origins, and a bookcase. In the kitchen there was a dinette table and two chairs. And in the bedroom there was a bed stripped down to mattress and box springs, one nightstand, and a dresser.

It would've been a pretty drab and impersonal place if it hadn't been for the photographs. There were dozens of them on the walls in every room including the bathroom, all black-and-white posed and candid shots of ferryboats and their crews dating back to the 1800s. Holdouts from his collection, I supposed. The photos created a nostalgic atmosphere, but there was also a certain sadness in the overall effect — glimpses of times and a way of life long gone, and a reminder that the man who had gathered them and been part of those times and ways was gone, too.

I started my search in the bedroom.

Poking through other people's possessions is uneasy work, and when the owner is deceased the task has a ghoulish feel. Besides, I had nothing specific to hunt for. So I was not quite as methodical as I might've been in different circumstances.

The nightstand yielded a well-used Bible, a rosary, and a spare dental plate in a plastic box. The dresser was less than half filled with underwear, socks, laundered shirts — and facedown in the bottom drawer, a framed and washed-out color photo of a heavyset, attractive young woman with curly blond hair. An inscription at the bottom read "To Archie — Love, Delia." It was at least fifty years old and the glass was cracked and webbed at the top, as if it had been smacked with something hard. According to Cybil, Captain Archie had never married. An unrequited love, and the glass broken in anger or frustration? Why keep the photo then, turned facedown in a bottom dresser drawer? One of those little pieces of a person's life that stir your imagination. And that made me feel the sadness again.

No hidey holes in the bedroom. Nothing taped under drawers or behind dresser, nightstand, headboard. Nothing hidden between mattress and box springs. I moved on to the bathroom. In the medicine cabinet I found a half-full bottle of small orange pills. Archie Todd's heart medicine, prescribed by Dr. Johannsen. The only other thing I found out from the cabinet was that Captain Archie had shaved with an old-fashioned straight razor.

Nothing of interest in the kitchen. The living room bookcase contained a few dozen beat-up paperback Western and historical novels, and half as many nonfiction texts on ferryboating. One of the texts, *Lore of the Ferrymen,* looked pretty old; I plucked it out, opened it to the copyright page. Published in 1891. As I started to put it back, I noticed writing on a scrap of paper that had been used as a bookmark. I slipped the paper free.

One word, Inca or Inco — I couldn't quite make out the last letter — and a telephone number, penned in a crabbed hand. The paper was white, with no signs of age; the phone prefix indicated it might be a San Francisco number. I tucked the scrap into my shirt pocket. Relevant or not, I would show it to Cybil as proof that I was every bit as thorough and sharp-eyed as Samuel Leatherman.

I'd saved the desk for last. The usual miscellany that accumulates in desk drawers; plain envelopes jammed with bill receipts marked Paid; bank envelopes bound together with a thick rubber band, each containing statements and a few cancelled checks written in the same crabbed hand. I found the three most recent statements and thumbed through the checks. Redwood Village, Dr. Johannsen, a local pharmacy, a supermarket, a credit card company. None were made out to individuals. I glanced at the statements. A deposit had been made on the first of each month in the amount of $2,500 — either a draw from his stock portfolio or a pension payment, because the amount was too large for a social security check. Most of the $2,500 went for rent; gracious retirement living in Redwood Village didn't come cheap. The average balance was in the $1,500 range, slightly more than that as of the latest statement.

Nothing.

I rummaged through the rest of the drawers. No personal correspondence of any kind. No copy of his will. No address book or Rolodex; if he'd had one of either, it had probably been turned over to the attorney, Evan Patterson. The only odd note was the absence of any account statements of other mailings from Dunbar Asset Management. There ought to be a fairly large file, given the size of Captain Archie's portfolio. Chances were they'd been turned over to

Evan Patterson as well, though why he would want all but the most recent —

"You there!" a voice said behind me, so suddenly and with such forcefulness that I twisted around, banged my knee, and nearly knocked over the desk. "What do you think you're doing?"

9

It was a woman, a big woman because she pretty much filled the open doorway. I hadn't heard the door open; I must not have closed it tightly when I let myself in, the afternoon breeze had blown it open, and I'd been too intent on my search to notice. She was back-lit by sunlight, so I couldn't tell much about her at first except her size.

"I asked what you're doing here." Gravelly voice, the kind that brooks no nonsense.

When you get caught with your drawers down or your hand in a cookie jar, the smart thing to do is to play dumb and bluff it out. I pasted on a sheepish smile and said, "Doing a favor for my mother-in-law. I should've known better."

"That's right, you should have." She came inside and a little to one side, so that I had a clearer look at her. Mid-forties, gray-streaked blond hair, a prominent nose. And

130

big all over, more bone and muscle than fat
— nearly six feet and a solid hundred and
sixty pounds, with a chest that strained the
front of her white blouse and probably required a D cup. "Just how did you get in?"

"She gave me a key. My mother-in-law."

"That's against the rules. If she has a key
to Mr. Todd's unit, she should have turned it
in after he died. What's her name?"

"Cybil Wade. The cottage across — "

"Oh, the writer. What's your name?"

I told her. Only that, not my profession.

"I'm Jocelyn Dunn, one of the nurses
here. What're you looking for?"

I was ready for that. I said, "Two chapters
of her new novel, the one she's writing now.
She can't find them and she thinks she may
have given them to Captain Archie to read
before he died. That's Cybil for you.
Absentminded as all get out."

"Did you find the chapters?"

"No. They're not in the desk. Maybe the
bedroom — "

"I'll look. You wait outside. Then we'll go
over and talk to Mrs. Wade."

I waited outside. Pretty soon Ms. Dunn
came out and said, "No manuscript pages
that I can see." Then she said, "The key,
please."

"Well, it is Cybil's . . ."

"No, it's not. It's the property of Redwood Village. The key, please. I'll lock the door."

I didn't have much choice; I gave her the key. She locked up and tucked the key into her pocket, and we went across the street to Cybil's duplex. I knocked on the door before I opened it, called out, "Company!" and did the ungentlemanly thing of going in first. Nurse Dunn didn't wait for an invitation; she came right in after me.

Kerry and Cybil were on the couch, drinking coffee. I said, "Cybil, I didn't find those two chapters from your manuscript. You must've misplaced them here somewhere."

She was a quick study. Without missing a beat she said, "Oh, dear. And I've torn the place apart. Hello, Nurse Dunn."

"Mrs. Wade, I'm surprised at you. Keeping a key to Archie Todd's unit and then sending your son-in-law over there to trespass. I really ought to report you."

Cybil managed to look contrite, and her apology was a model of false sincerity. Nurse Dunn relented, lectured Cybil on abiding by the rules, and then took her big hide out of there and left the three of us alone.

Cybil, reproachfully: "So you got caught."

Me, defensively: "Nobody's perfect. Not even that fictional superdick of yours."

"Did you find anything before the side of beef spotted you?"

"Probably not. Unless this means something to you." I showed her the scrap of paper. "It was in one of his books."

"Inca? No, nothing."

"Last letter could be an 'o.' Inco."

"I never heard Archie use either word."

"Well, let's see what calling the number gets us."

It didn't get us a thing. San Francisco number, all right, but it had been disconnected.

"Monday," I said. "This, Evan Patterson, whatever else I can do. Just don't expect much to come of it, okay?"

"I don't," Cybil said. "I didn't when I decided to hire you."

Which may or may not have been a mild shot. With Cybil you can't always tell. She likes me, I think she respects me, but down deep she's never quite forgiven me for not living up to her Samuel Leatherman ideal of the tough and infallible private eye.

When the phone rang at six-thirty that evening I was trying to relax by watching a forties film noir on TV. *The Web*, with Edmond O'Brien. Pretty good, but my head wasn't into it. Cybil kept intruding; so did little Emily Hunter.

Kerry answered the call and sang out that it was for me. I went to take it on the kitchen phone.

A male voice said angrily, "She's gone, goddamn it. You may as well know."

"Who's gone? Who is this?"

"Trevor Smith. You know damn well who's gone."

"Sheila Hunter?"

"And her kid. Both of them."

I could hear my breath in my throat; it had a ground-glass sound. "Gone where?"

"She wouldn't tell me."

"When?"

"Yesterday afternoon sometime."

"And you waited this long to call me?"

"She told me not to tell anybody, particularly you. I wasn't going to, but . . . ah, Christ, I don't know what to do."

"Gone away for a while, or — ?"

"Two or three weeks, she said. Someplace where she can pull herself together. But I don't know . . . the way the two of them acted Thursday night, the way Sheila put me off on the phone yesterday, I don't think they're coming back."

"Easy, back up a little. What happened — "

"Don't tell me to take it easy," he

134

snapped. "You and your investigation, harassing her . . . this is *your* fault. If you'd just left her alone . . ."

"I'll take the blame if you want to lay it on me. But the truth is, she's running because of whatever she and her husband were mixed up in ten years ago."

I listened to silence for eight or ten beats. He used the time to get a grip on himself; he sounded calmer when he said, "She claims you're crazy, that she and Jack had a perfectly normal life in Pennsylvania before they moved out here."

"And you believe her."

More dead air, about five beats' worth this time. "I don't know what to believe," he said.

"You tell her what I said about helping her?"

"I told her. She called you a liar and a lot worse."

"How scared was she?"

"*Scared,* man. She nearly had a hemorrhage when I said that damn word to her."

"What word? Crazybone?"

"She turned white. I thought she was going to keel over."

"Give you any idea what it means?"

"No. I tried to get it out of her, but she — Don't you know?"

135

"No idea."

"Then where'd you get it?"

I told him about startling her in the potting shed on Tuesday. "It has a pretty terrible meaning for her, whatever it is. It's tied to the reason she ran away."

"Yeah," Smith said. Then he said, "I think she was already planning to go before I showed up."

"Thursday night, you mean. At her house."

"Yeah. She didn't say anything about leaving then, not until she called me at home yesterday — I took the day off work, waited around, I thought she might need me. I didn't think she'd just run out of my life, I thought we had something better than that . . ." The last couple of words had a phlegmy sound, as if he were choking up. He drew an audible breath. "I wanted to marry her," he said then. "I still do."

There was nothing for me to say to that. I asked, "What makes you think she'd already made up her mind to run?"

"How uptight she was before I even mentioned you. Uptight and scared. Emily, too. Both of them."

"Was Emily there when you talked to Sheila?"

"No. Crying in her bedroom by then."

"Crying? Why was she crying?"

"Sheila . . . smacked her, that's why."

My hand tightened around the receiver. "Hurt her?"

"No. Slap across the face. She's got a temper, a bad temper when she's upset, and the kid wouldn't leave the room. She knew something was going on . . . Emily did . . . and she wanted to know what it was."

"And you just let her mother hit her?"

"I'd've stopped it if I could. It happened too quick. You think I like the idea of kids being smacked around? Well, I don't."

"All right. Is she in the habit of hitting her daughter?"

"I don't think so. No."

"Ever see Emily with bruises or marks?"

"No. Christ, Sheila's not like that. She's *not*, dammit. It's just that Jack getting killed, the two of us seeing each other, this thing she's so afraid of . . . everything coming down on her at once, it's got her half crazy."

No damn excuse, I thought, but I didn't say it. I said, "What about the two of you? Going on how long?"

"What the hell does that matter?"

"How long, Trevor?"

"Three months. That's all I'm going to say about Sheila and me."

"How about her husband? He played

around, too, didn't he?"

"Damn right he did. Why do you think Sheila — Never mind, I'm not getting into that either." He sucked in another audible breath. "Listen, you're a detective, you've got your nose in this already. You think you can find her?"

"I'm sure going to try." But not for your sake or hers, I thought. For Emily's. "Did she ever mention anyone named Karen to you? Artist, makes stained glass, lives somewhere up the coast."

"No. A friend of hers?"

"Or a relative. Emily calls her Aunt Karen."

"Sheila didn't talk much about her personal life," Smith said. "Didn't have any relatives in California or anywhere else that I know about."

"Okay. They left yesterday afternoon, you said?"

"Before two. It was after one when she called me. Said she was leaving, told me not to tell anybody, don't talk to you at all anymore — she'd be in touch. I said wait, let me come over, we'll talk it over first, but her mind was made up. As soon as we hung up I drove up to her house. I live in Santa Clara, it took me forty minutes to get there. They were already gone by then. I stayed home today, too, I thought maybe she'd call. When she didn't . . . I had to talk to somebody, I couldn't just sit around and wait for a call that might never come . . ."

"You did the right thing contacting me. Where will you be tomorrow?"

"Emerald Hills. Another day here and I'll go nuts."

"All right. I'll see what I can find out. Call you if there's any news."

"Yeah, thanks." Pause. "I don't blame you. The kind of trouble Shiela must be in . . ." Another pause. "Shit," he said.

Yes, I thought, and the pile keeps getting bigger. And I wish I knew where to find a shovel.

I couldn't sleep.

I kept lying there with my eyes wide open, watching the dark and listening to Kerry's even breathing and thinking mostly about Emily Hunter. Her mother had overheard part of her call to me, or found out about it some other way; that was why she hadn't shown up at the riding academy. It was also why Sheila Hunter had decided to pack up the kid, ripping out ten years' worth of roots, and haul her off to Christ knew where. Bad trouble, all right, but it wasn't just the woman's anymore. She'd made it her daughter's as well. Ten years old, sensitive, bewildered . . . *did* Emily have any idea of what it was all about? If she did, it wasn't because her mother had confided in her. The only secret-sharing Mrs. Hunter had done was with her late husband and co-conspirator. And yet the Hunters' relationship couldn't have been all that tightly bound after a decade, else both of them wouldn't have been seeking solace in other people's beds. How long had they been cheating on each other? Recent thing, or had the marriage begun to unravel long ago from too much guilt, too much fear?

Crazybone. The word was at or near the center of the Hunters' secret, of Sheila's panicked flight. But without some connection, some piece of the hidden past, there was no way to decipher it.

A nonsense jingle began to run around inside my head; kept on running until fatigue drove me down into a restless sleep. Crazybone connected to the shoulder bone, shoulder bone connected to the neck bone, neck bone connected to the crazybone, and little Emily's gone away . . .

10

On a Sunday morning the sleepy country-village atmosphere of Greenwood was even more pronounced. The main drag and side streets were mostly deserted, and what cars I encountered and what people I saw seemed to be on their way to and from church. A large contingent of worshippers was exiting the one church I passed, all of them well dressed. It was good to see that the old-fashioned standard of Sunday wear still applied in places like this. A surprisingly large percentage of churchgoers these days thought nothing of attending services in jeans and sweatshirts and the like. Meaning no disrespect, just making the statement that they didn't see any good reason to dress up for the occasion. God didn't run a fashion agency, so did He really care what His flock was outfitted in when they offered up their prayers?

The new breed had a point, but as a member of the old breed I preferred the upholding of tradition. Hypocritical member of the old breed, it could be argued, since I seldom attended Mass anymore, but so be it. Besides, formalized religion and strict interpretation of biblical doctrine don't necessarily make a good Christian — a fact some radical members of the Religious Right would do well to recognize. A person's relationship with God is or ought to be a personal and private thing. If individuals want to worship in a group, fine; if they prefer to worship alone and in their own fashion, fine. The world would be a far better place if people would stop trying to tell others what to believe and how to believe in it, in religious and other matters.

A sharpening breeze created a rippling effect in Whiskey Flat Road's tree tunnel, so that branches and trunks seemed to be flowing around the car as I drove through. The motile illusion bothered my eyes, even though I was wearing sunglasses. So did the bright sunlight down here, it being another perfect day in this pocket paradise. Too little sleep last night and too much eyestrain over the course of nearly sixty years. Kerry had been after me to make an appointment with an optometrist — and I kept putting it off because I was afraid he'd tell me I needed to wear glasses all the time instead of just for reading.

The gates were still open at the foot of the Hunters' driveway, so I swung in between the pillars without slowing. The parking area above was tenanted by nothing more than a scatter of leaves. I parked among them, got out and stood for a few seconds looking around. Except for all the house windows being draped, blinded, or shuttered, everything appeared pretty much the same as on my first visit. And why shouldn't it? I thought irritably. Abandonment didn't change the outward look of things, just the feel of them.

A red light bloomed on a key plate set into the porch wall, an announcement that the alarm system was armed. Even if I yielded to an impulse to jimmy my way through a locked door or window, I couldn't do it without setting off the alarm. That wouldn't have stopped Samuel Leatherman; he'd have bulled his way inside, discovered an important clue in two or three minutes, and been long gone before a security patrol or police car showed up. But I wasn't Samuel Leatherman, and glad of it in spite of dear old Cybil. Chances were, Sheila Hunter hadn't left any clues behind anyway.

I walked around the house to her potting studio, more for the exercise than with any purpose. Locked up as tight as the house. No alarm system here, and none needed. This was where she'd come to get away from her troubles; she wouldn't keep reminders of the past around. Just the same I took a quick look through the glass wall. Tuesday's tableau minus Mrs. Hunter, the clay in the tubs as cold as her dead husband.

Back the way I'd come and across to the detached garage. The double doors were locked and so was a side door; the only window had a shade drawn so tightly over it I couldn't see inside. Alarm system on the house, shade on the garage window, and weapons somewhere on the premises, no doubt. Suburban paranoia had nothing to do with it, either. Damn safe bet somebody, somewhere, really had been after the Hunters for the past ten years.

An idea occurred to me on the way to the car. I fired up the engine and coasted down to the foot of the drive. Whiskey Flat Road was deserted, so I set the brake and got out again and went to the mailbox, which was attached to the inside of one of the pillars; there was a slot on the outside so mail could be put through when the gates were shut. The box wasn't locked and there was mail inside, all right — yesterday's delivery, at least. I fished it out. Two catalogues, three pieces of junk, and a PG&E bill. So much for my brainstorm. Like a lot of my clever little ideas, it was a practical bust.

The wind made chuckling sounds in the trees as I returned to the car. Or maybe it was that rough, tough action hero, Sam Leatherman, laughing at me from somewhere up in pulp heaven.

As I drove toward the village, something began bothering me — a nagging little irritation at the back of my mind. It was not clear enough to identify, and I couldn't seem to catch hold of it. Something I'd seen or hadn't seen or should have seen at the Hunter place; something that was off in some small way. Might be significant and might not. I'd have to figure out what it was before I could tell.

Come to me sooner or later. Picking at it would only drive it in deeper.

Anita Purcell had returned from her trip to L.A.; she was just opening her fine arts shop when I got there. She was short, gray-haired, energetic, and steely-eyed, and as I might have predicted, she didn't want anything to do with me or my ilk. Those were almost her exact words when I introduced myself: "I want nothing to do with you or your ilk."

I was tempted to ask her what she thought my ilk was. Instead I said, "Well, I'm sorry you feel that way, Ms. Purcell. But you may have information about Sheila Hunter — "

"You'll get no information from me."

"Your niece told me you — "

"My niece had no business telling you anything. She won't make that mistake again."

Which meant that Gretchen Kiley had 'fessed up and her aunt knew all about my previous visit. Closed issue, as far as Ms. Purcell was concerned. I made one more stab at trying to pry it open.

"What would you say if I told you Mrs. Hunter and her daughter left Greenwood suddenly on Friday and won't be coming back?"

The steely eyes had heat in them, like metal in a forge. "Yes? If that's true, and I doubt it is, you're responsible for driving them away. You and your hounding and bullying."

"Is that what she told you? That I was hounding her?"

"Do you deny it?"

"She's in trouble," I said. "She and Emily both."

"What kind of trouble could a grieving widow and a little girl be in that wasn't generated by you and your employer?"

"I'm not sure of the specifics. All I know is — "

"Nonsense. That kind of talk cuts no ice with me."

"It isn't nonsense. I'm not looking to harm the Hunters, I'm trying to help them. And I can't do that unless you help me find out where they went. It's possible Mrs. Hunter confided in or is staying with a woman named Karen, a stained-glass artist who lives somewhere up the coast. All I'm asking is any information you may have about this woman. Her full name, a telephone number — "

"My God," she said, "what amazing gall you have. If I weren't a lady, I'd tell you what else I think you're full of."

Hopeless. Sheila Hunter had planted an image of me as the relentless pursuer in Ms. Purcell's mind, one enhanced by what she considered to be the profligate tongue of her niece, and no amount of appeal, disclosure, or wheedling was going to change it. There was nothing for me to do but take what she thought I was full of away to dump on somebody else.

Sunday was a big day at Emerald Hills Country Club. Both tiers of the parking lot were jammed; I had to leave my car with a few other late arrivals along the edge of the entrance drive, a good three hundred yards from the main building. Not all of the cars would belong to golfers, although men and women and carts littered what I could see of the fairways and greens. Brunchers, lunchers, social drinkers, serious drinkers, and kibitzers would be plentiful, too.

A different guy was manning the security desk this morning, just as polite and not quite as supercilious. He let me sign in and pass by with a minimum of scrutiny. I went first to the Greens Room, on the chance that I might find Dale Cooney alone and getting an early start at the bar. No such luck; she wasn't anywhere in the room. So I'd have to try to brace her at home after all, a gloomy prospect but a necessary one if I was going to get anything out of her today.

Outside, the terrace was packed with people eating and paying little or no attention to a string quartet that was making pretty music on the far side. I went down the steps and started along the path to the pro shop. Three men in golf togs were coming toward me, two of them in animated conversation and the third a couple of paces behind with his head down and his face set in brooding lines. The lagger was the self-proclaimed guiltless dentist, Doc Lukash.

I eased over and cut between the two talkers and Lukash, so that he was forced to pull up short to keep from running into me. I said through a friendly smile, "Morning, Doctor."

He looked at me blankly for three or four seconds. Recognition, when it came, dragged his thin mouth and chin down even further, out of a brood into a scowl. "Oh, it's you," he said. "What're you doing here?"

"Talking to people. You have a bad round?"

"What?"

"Your golf game. You don't seem very happy this morning."

"Neither my golf game nor my mood is any of your business. Are you still investigating Sheila Hunter, for God's sake?"

"That's right. And with more reason now than before."

"What are you talking about?"

"She's left town. Looks like she won't be coming back."

". . . I don't believe you."

"Truth, so help me."

"Why would she do that? Unless you had

something to do with it . . ."

"I had something to do with it, yes, but that's not the main reason she left. She's got troubles, big troubles. Something that happened years ago, before she moved to Greenwood."

"Something . . . what trouble? What happened?"

"Don't you know?"

"I have no idea. How would I know?"

"Well, you were pretty close to her once. I thought maybe she — "

He bristled. Part of it was a pose of indignation, but underneath there was a tremulous emotion that might have been fear. "I told you before," he said, "I have never been involved with Sheila Hunter, romantically or otherwise. Malicious gossip, that's all it is. If you repeat it, if you bother me again, I'll sue you and that insurance company of yours for harassment and slander. Is that clear?"

"Clear enough."

He stepped around me and headed for the steps, moving in that slow, jerky way of people under tight restraint — as if he'd rather have run than walked away from me.

Just what are you afraid of, Doctor? I thought. Your reputation? Or is it something you know about Sheila Hunter's past that you wish you didn't?

I went on to the pro shop. Trevor Smith wasn't there; the tow-headed kid behind the counter said he was out on the links, giving a lesson to one of the members, and that he wouldn't be back until around twelve-thirty. Fine, dandy. Now I had another forty-five minutes or so to kill.

I wandered back inside the main building. A quick lunch would have been good, even at Emerald Hills' prices, but reservations were probably required and a non-member would have trouble getting a table anyway. Into the Greens Room again. Still no sign of Dale Cooney. Lukash was in there drinking his lunch, but he wasn't alone, and I wouldn't have bothered him again if he was — not just yet. I managed to carve a piece of standing room at the bar, where I had an elegant lunch of a Bud Light and a handful of salted nuts and pretzel sticks. The beer cost five dollars, just about the price of an entire six-pack where Kerry and I did our shopping. By the time twelve-thirty rolled around, I was in a mood to, in that good old pro football cliché, kick some serious butt.

Trevor Smith showed up in the pro-shop at twelve-forty. He looked hopeful when he first saw me, then worried by my expression, and finally resigned when I took him aside and told him I hadn't found out anything yet. "Information's the reason I'm here," I said.

"What kind of information?"

"For one thing, an address for Dale Cooney."

"Mrs. Cooney? What do you want with her?"

"She was having an affair with Jack Hunter. Pretty serious, from what I gather. Maybe he was less careful about letting something slip in the sack than his wife was."

Smith said with a flare of anger, "That's damn crude."

"All right, maybe it was. But none of this business is of high moral caliber and I don't feel like being polite about it anymore. With you or anybody else. Can you tell me where Dale Cooney lives?"

"Yes," he said, thin-lipped. "Burnt Leaf Road, not far from here. I don't know the number but I'll find out."

"You do that. But first, answer some questions about Doc Lukash."

Caught him off guard again. "What about Mr. Lukash?"

"Did he have an affair with Sheila?"

Smith made a grinding noise with his teeth.

"Come on, now," I said. "*Was* he one of her lovers?"

"You make it sound as if she had a whole string — "

"Yes or no?"

"No. There was some gossip about it a while back, before Sheila and I got together, but that's all it was."

"How do you know that's all it was?"

"Sheila said so. I asked her . . . I wanted to know . . . and she said absolutely not. He made a pass at her, more than one, but she wouldn't have anything to do with him. I believe her."

That makes one of us, I thought. As if people who cheat on their spouses never lie; as if the current occupant of the White House never lied. "What can you tell me about Lukash? Married, family man?"

"Yes. Wife and two sons, both at Stanford."

"What is euphemistically known as happily married?"

"I don't see how, if he's making passes at other women. Besides, his wife's a bitch."

"Yes?"

"Bosses him around. Bosses everybody around."

"So he's a chaser."

Smith shrugged. "The only gossip I've

153

heard is the crap about him and Sheila."

"What would his wife do if she caught him cheating?"

"Divorce him. Or Bobbittize him. She's the type."

So maybe that's what's scaring him, I thought. Doesn't want the wife to find out about the lust in his heart for Sheila Hunter, requited or not.

I said, "Back to Sheila. If she wasn't seeing Lukash, who was she seeing before you?"

He ground his teeth again. "Nobody."

"No gossip about her and anybody else?"

"There's always gossip floating around here."

"Linking her and which men?"

"Listen, I don't want — "

"I do want. Names, Trevor."

"Why? The men . . . they don't know anything about where she and Emily went."

"Let me find that out for myself."

"Cheap gossip, that's all it is. You just remember that."

I waited.

"All right." He spat three names at me as if they were a bad taste in his mouth.

"They all live in Greenwood?" He nodded, and I said, "I'll need addresses for them, too. And occupations and anything

154

else you can tell me so I'll have some idea of who I'm dealing with if I have to talk to them."

"*If?*"

"I won't do it except as a last resort. And if I do, I won't mention you."

"Is that supposed to make me feel better?"

"Look," I said, "the bottom line here is that I'm on your side and Sheila and her daughter's side. I think I told you that before. Don't make me say it again."

"Okay," he said heavily. "Okay. I'm worried about her, that's all."

"Believe it or not, so am I."

"I'll get those addresses."

11

Burnt Leaf Road was a snaky passage that led up into the hills. Dale Cooney had told Charles, the bartender, that she lived exactly one mile from the country club. Not so, according to my odometer, which measured the distance at 1.1 miles. Maybe the odometer in her Mercedes was off; mine had always been reliable. Or maybe she'd just rounded off the number for convenience or because it sounded better and what the hell did it matter anyway? Only somebody like me would even notice a thing like that and then ponder it as if it were one of life's weighty issues.

There was a brick arch over the entrance to the driveway, an iffy proposition in earthquake country, though the bricks were moss-studded and looked old enough to have survived most big shakes since 1906. I drove on through and down a long gradual slope. The house, brick and rough-hewn wood, was also close to being a centenarian; it sat on a flat section, natural or man-made I couldn't tell, about halfway down. Below it the slope was steeper and ended at a narrow creek and a section of dense woods. Over the tops of the trees I could see all the way to San Francisco Bay in the hazy distance. You'd have the same wide-angle view from inside the house.

A garage large enough for three cars sat off to the left. I parked a short distance in front of it and stepped out into a woodsy silence punctuated by birdsong. A redwood-bark path led me to the house. I had a story ready in the event Frank Cooney answered the door; if it was Dale Cooney, I'd arrange to meet her somewhere and make sure she understood that I meant business.

All well and good, except that nobody responded to the door chimes.

Now what?

I could hang around Greenwood and come back later, or I could leave a note, or I could set up a meeting by phone at some point. None of the choices had much appeal. I leaned on the bell again, mainly out of frustration, and the lack of response only increased it. Grumbling, I returned to the car.

Something caught my attention as I opened the door — a faint acrid smell that didn't belong with the sweet woods flavor. I stood with my head up, sniffing like a hound. Faint, and familiar. Too familiar. I looked over at the garage. And the skin began to crawl on the back of my scalp, a sensation that worsened when I started over that way. Coming from inside the garage, all right.

There were no outside handles on the double doors: electronically controlled and locked down tight. No window or door on the near side; I ran around on the downhill side. Door there, but it was locked or jammed. Alongside it was a window, unshaded and unobstructed. When I put my face up close to the glass I had a dim view of the interior.

Gray haze filled it, the deadly kind I'd seen once before on a case. Through its puffy, hanging layers I could make out one car, Dale Cooney's Mercedes, its top still down. Somebody was behind the wheel, head thrown back and to one side; I thought it was a woman but I couldn't be sure.

I broke the window with my elbow. The seal in there must have been pretty tight; stinking carbon monoxide fumes came pouring out, driving me back and to one side. I went along the wall to the door and threw my weight against it. Jammed, not locked — it gave inward, scraping along the cement floor. I kicked it all the way open, releasing more of the gray poison, and then ran over to the house and hunted up a hose bib and soaked my handkerchief in cold water. Back to the garage, where the outpour through door and window had thinned. I took a couple of deep, slow breaths, held the wet handkerchief over my mouth and nose, and ducked inside.

The woman in the car was Dale Cooney. Dead — long dead. Her face was a bright, shiny cherry red.

The monoxide was in my lungs in spite of the handkerchief, tearing loose coughs and making me lightheaded. I got out of there into the fresh air, stood sucking it with my head down until I could breathe all right again. Then I hurried to the car, glanced at the mobile phone, unclipped the flashlight from under the dash instead. No hurry in making a 911 call. And there was something I wanted to check on first, something I'd noticed when I peered at the woman's face up close.

I soaked the handkerchief again before I returned to the garage. The air in there was better now but still not breathable. I switched the flash on, held the beam on her face. Her eyes, wide open with the pupils rolled up, were like iridescent milk-glass in the beam; her mouth hung open, a ghastly rictus. I tasted bile in my throat, but it didn't keep me from using the edge of the flash to gently turn her face toward me. Her head moved loosely on the stem of her neck — and when I touched and then lifted one of her hands, it felt cold, rubbery. Rigor had come and gone; she'd been dead since last night, maybe even yesterday afternoon.

On the seat beside the body was a leather handbag, a remote-control garage door opener, and a half-empty bottle of Speyburn single malt Scotch. Both the car and the dead woman reeked of whiskey. I checked the floor and the shelf seat in back; they were empty. Before I clicked off the flash and got out of there I took note of what she was wearing: expensive dark brown pants suit, the jacket adorned with an elaborate turquoise pin, and a full complement of lipstick and makeup. Out somewhere before this happened that required looking her best.

Outside I filled up on oxygen again. I had a brief flashback image of Dale Cooney walking out of the Greens Room, stiff and straight and on her dignity; it brought the taste of sickness back into my throat. Maintaining dignity, not making a spectacle of herself, had been important to her. There were few worse ways for a person like that to die.

When my lungs quit hurting I went to the car and put in the 911 call. I would have preferred to drive away from there and make the call anonymously from a pay phone — now more than before, after what I'd seen in the garage. But I couldn't do it. Ethics, duty. And the fact that I was already involved, with one part of her life and possibly with her death as well.

On the surface it seemed simple enough. Alcoholic drives home drunk, nipping on a bottle of Scotch on the way; makes it inside her garage, presses the button to lower the door, then passes out with the engine still running. Tragic accident. Happens all the time.

Except that I doubted it had happened that way in this case. The thing had a staged feel. And the bruised area I'd seen on the side of her head, just above the hairline, said she might've been slugged unconscious before her lungs started to fill with carbon monoxide.

Not an accident — murder.

Motive related to the Hunters in some

way? Something she knew about their past, something Jack Hunter had told her? If so, it made this whole business a hell of a lot more sinister and deadly than I'd imagined.

The local cops were polite and no more suspicious or adversarial than most law-enforcement officials when dealing with a private investigator. They did keep me hanging and rattling for more than two hours, answering the same questions from different minions, but it was professionally handled all the way. I told them exactly why I'd come to see Mrs. Cooney, about my talk with her at the country club, about the investigation I was conducting for Intercoastal Insurance. The only things I held back were my suspicions about the Hunters' past and of the nature of Dale Cooney's death. It was not my place to call attention to the bruise on her temple; they'd spot it themselves, or the coroner would, and interpret it however they saw fit. The quickest way to antagonize public officials is to try to tell them their business. Cooperate and otherwise keep your own counsel, and cordial relations can usually be maintained for the duration.

Another smart thing to do is to keep your ears open while your mouth is shut. I found out that Frank Cooney was away on a business trip, had left last Friday for New York; one of the cops got that information from a neighbor and passed it on in my hearing. I also learned that the Cooneys lived alone, no children or relatives or in-home domestic help. So it wasn't surprising that Dale Cooney hadn't been found until I showed up. And the fact that she'd been here alone for the weekend, coupled with the property's relative isolation, would have made it easy for somebody to put her and her Mercedes into the garage, and take his — or her — time arranging things to look like an accident.

Who? Sheila Hunter? Most likely suspect, if the motive was connected to her hidden past. Except that she'd been on the run with Emily since Friday afternoon . . .

Or had she?

The gates at the foot of the driveway — that was the thing about the Hunter place that had been bothering me. Why were the gates still open when everything else was closed up tight and the alarm system turned on?

It came to me after the Greenwood police let me go, as I was rolling away from the Cooney property. I drove straight across the village to Whiskey Flat Road. The gates were

163

still open, and it didn't look as though anyone had been through them since my earlier visit. To make sure I was alone I walked close enough to the house to see that the alarm system was still activated. Then I veered over to the garage.

I was conscious of a tightness in my chest and across my shoulders as I approached the side door. Sharp in my mind was the picture of Dale Cooney's corpse, head flung back, eyes milk-white, mouth in rictus, skin that hideous cherry red. If I had to look at a sight like that twice in one day . . .

No smell of exhaust fumes here; I took several deep breaths to be certain. The door was still locked. I bent to peer at the knob and locking plate. Push-button, not a dead bolt, and the fit didn't appear to be tight. I went to work with one of my credit cards. More often than not, despite what Hollywood would have you believe, that kind of maneuvering gets you nothing but frustrated; and if it does work, it takes a lot longer than three or four seconds to pop the bolt. But I got lucky in both categories: the card trick not only worked, it took me less than four minutes.

I sucked in a breath before I pushed the door all the way open and poked my head inside. The air in there was clear, no trace of monoxide, but there was a car parked in the gloom — big, dark-colored. I went in and along the driver's side to peer through the window.

Empty, front and back.

I let the breath out and tried the door. Open. I leaned in and felt along the front seat without finding anything. The glove compartment yielded three packets of tissues, a couple of pieces of hard candy, a bundle of maps, and not much else — no registration or insurance papers, nothing to identify the owner. I found the trunk release and went and looked in there. Nothing.

The car was a new or nearly new Audi, four-door, maroon with a black interior. The license plate wasn't personalized; I made a mental note of the number. Then I went back outside, shutting the door but leaving it unlocked.

In my car I called Emerald Hills. Trevor Smith was in the pro shop; he answered right away.

"Any word from Sheila Hunter?" I asked him.

"No. Nothing. But I heard about you finding Mrs. Cooney dead in her garage — it's all over the club. What — "

"Never mind about that now. What kind of car does Mrs. Hunter drive?"

"Why do you want to know that?"

"Answer the question."

"An Audi. New this year."

"Color?"

"Dark red. Maroon."

"Is that the only car she owns?"

"Yeah. Listen, why are you asking about her car? You find out where she went?"

"Not yet. Working an angle, that's all."

"You'd better not be holding out on me — "

"I'll be in touch," I said, and broke the connection.

So where was she? Had she and Emily left here with someone else on Friday? Or had they gone in her car and she'd come back for some reason, alone or with the kid, then left again with someone else? Was Emily still with her or not?

Dammit, I didn't like this. Mother and daughter missing was bad enough, but the complications made it even more disturbing. There had to be a third party involved — the Audi in the garage said so, and Dale Cooney's sudden death pointed that way.

Who? And how did he or she fit in?

12

At the office Monday morning I gave Tamara a couple of research jobs to work on first thing. Number one priority was to try to get a line on the woman named Karen, the stained-glass artist, through North Coast galleries, antique collectives, artists' associations, and the like. The task was one I should've put her on on Friday — but until Trevor Smith's call and the events of yesterday, it hadn't seemed urgent. Now it was. Karen's identity was the only lead I had to Emily and her mother, and at that it was a tenuous one.

As good as Tamara was with the computer, her chance of success depended on a number of intangibles. First, on whether Karen was the woman's real name — Emily calling her "Aunt Karen" wasn't proof of that or of a blood relationship. And even if it was her real name, she might not use it to

sign her work. There there was how successful and well-known she was, whether she
was a joiner, whether she displayed her
pieces in galleries or other retail outlets. If
she happened to have a website, she'd be
easy to locate. If she was a contract artist
working for a manufacturer or a wholesaler,
or a hobbyist whose creations were limited
to a few pieces for herself, relatives, friends,
she might be damn difficult to track down.

Tamara's second job was Cybil-related:
Find out who or what Inca or Inco was,
when the San Francisco phone number had
been disconnected, the name of the person
representing Inca/Inco (if in fact it was a
company or organization) who had applied
for the phone number in the first place, and
the billing address. That one should be easy
enough when she got around to it. Tamara
had developed a cyber contact in Pac Bell's
main office, and it had taken her only a few
months to do it. Whereas I'd spent years es-
tablishing a personal contact there, using
what charm I possessed supplemented by
small bribes — and a couple of years ago my
contact had quit unexpectedly and moved to
Minneapolis. Good old technology. It even
simplified ethics bending.

I fidgeted at my desk while Tamara tapped
away on her Mac, paying a few bills and get-

ting a bank deposit ready. Then I went to work on the phone. I returned a couple of calls, one of which earned me a minor commission for an employee background check. It was after ten by then, so I rang up Emerald Hills and spoke briefly to Trevor Smith. Still no word from Sheila Hunter. Or if she had contacted him, he wasn't admitting it.

On impulse I punched out the Hunters' number. No answer; no answering machine. Was that Audi of hers still in the garage? Only way to find out was to drive down there, but I wasn't ready for that just yet. Wait a while, see how Tamara's searches shaped up.

I called Archie Todd's attorney, Evan Patterson. Not in the office yet. Some lawyers keep bankers' hours, I thought in my cynical fashion, and left my name and number. Dr. Leonard Johannsen next. He was in, and willing to answer my questions when I said they pertained to a routine insurance investigation. I didn't say anything about suspicious circumstances.

What the conversation amounted to was a medical confirmation and little else. No, there wasn't any reason for Archie Todd to have taken a larger dosage of digitoxin; his daily maintenance dose was sufficient and had in fact stabilized his condition. Now and then, Johannsen said, a patient would attempt self-medication, often with disastrous results, but Captain Archie had not been that kind of fool. And yes, a large dosage of the drug could easily induce a heart attack in a CHF patient. The peak toxic effects following an acute overdose could take up to twelve hours, but fatal ventricular fibrillation might happen a lot sooner, depending on the individual and the size of the overdose.

Tamara wasn't getting anywhere with the Karen search; she shook her head at me when I asked her. Restlessness prodded me out of the office and downstairs to see if the mail had come. The mailman was there and just putting it up. I sifted through mine as I went back upstairs.

Nothing much until I came to the next to last envelope. Handwritten address, no return address, and the handwriting had a careful, slanted roundness — more the hand of a child than an adult. I ripped open the envelope. Folded sheet of ruled paper torn from a notebook. When I opened the fold, something fell out: an address label, one of those small printed mail-order kind, torn off a red envelope.

I looked at the label first. The name on it

was K. Meineke; the address was 410 Port Creek Road, Gualala, CA.

Gualala. A little town on the coast, in southern Mendocino County. A town noted as something of an artists' haven, among its other attractions.

I opened the letter. The same careful writing filled both sides. The salutation was formal and the body of it read:

I'm writing this letter because my mom is watching the phone and she took away my pc so I can't e-mail you. She heard me making plans to meet you at the riding academy and locked me in my room. I don't know what else to do. I have a stamp and I'll try to sneak out and put this in our mailbox. I'll have to put up the red flag so the mailman will take it but maybe Mom won't notice.

We're going away. Running away, I guess. To Aunt Karen's first but I don't think we'll stay there very long. I don't know where we'll go after that. Mom won't tell me. Aunt Karen lives in Gualala. She sent me a birthday card a few days ago and I still have the envelope. I'll put her address label in here so you'll know where to find us.

I don't want to go. I tried to talk Mom into staying but she wouldn't listen. She's so scared she's acting crazy. She won't tell me why. The only thing she said was "If he finds me he'll kill me." I said who would. She said "Somebody I knew a long time ago, before you were born." She wouldn't tell me his name or where she knew him or why he wants to kill her.

I'm scared too. That's why I'm writing this letter to you. You're the only person I know who can help us. Mom doesn't think so but I do.

Please help us if you get this letter. Something bad is going to happen, I know it. I've already lost my dad, I don't want to lose my mom too.

It was signed "Sincerely, Emily Hunter."

Tightness in my throat and a bitter taste in my mouth when I finished reading it. You'd have to be a pretty hard case not to be moved by a letter like this.

Back in the office I said to Tamara, "You can quit the Karen hunt. I just found out who she is and where she lives."

"No lie? How?"

"This came in the mail."

"Some kid," Tamara said when she fin-

172

ished reading the letter. "Sure puts a lot of faith in you."

"Not too much, I hope."

"You be going to Gualala?"

"Have to. Even if they're not there I might be able to get something out of Karen Meineke. I can make it to Gualala by one-thirty or so. Not much more than a three-hour drive."

"Anything you want me to do?"

"One thing. If you're willing. Drive down to Greenwood and check out the Hunters' property. If nobody's there, look in the garage and see if Mrs. Hunter's Audi is still inside."

"Sure. Why wouldn't I be willing? More field work I get to do, the better I like it."

"Well . . ."

She gave me a slow, lopsided grin. "You worried about a black face getting too much attention down there?"

"Not that. You. I don't want you to get in trouble."

"Me? Trouble? Hey, man, I was born in Redwood City, remember? I knows all about how to deal wif rich white folks in dey fine homes." Her voice had risen to a shrill, grating parody of African-American speech. "Lawdy, I'se been comin' over cheer to do foh Miz Hunter and other folks foh a long

173

time now. Yassuh, nosuh, I wasn't doin' nothin' wrong, I sho' wasn't."

"I hate it when you do Butterfly McQueen."

"Not half as much as I hate black stereotypes."

"All right. Just don't lay it on too thick."

"You leave that to me."

"If Mrs. Hunter is home, or anybody else is there, make up an excuse and get away as quickly as you can. Don't tell anybody you work for me unless you have to."

"Boss," Tamara said, "quit fussin' and get movin'. I'm a big girl now. And I already have a daddy."

I was on Highway 1 between Jenner and Fort Bragg, the narrow, winding stretch that hugs the high cliffsides and gives height-fearing people like me sweaty palms, when the car phone buzzed. I negotiated another tight curve before I answered it.

"I'm down here in White Folks Heaven," Tamara said. "On my way out and back to the real world."

"No trouble?"

"Few looks, that's all. You know what I'm saying?"

"Yeah. What'd you find out?"

"Nobody home at the Hunters', alarm

system still on, big Audi sitting in the garage."

"Look like anyone's been there since yesterday?"

"Uh-uh. Got that deserted feel."

"Okay. Thanks, Tamara."

"What else you got for me to do?"

"Nothing on the Hunter case until I see what I can find out in Gualala. When you get back to the office, go ahead with the Pac Bell search — "

"Way ahead of you there. I e-mailed my man before I left and he already got back to me." She was a true child of the new age; she carried a laptop with her everywhere she went — to bed and the bathroom, for all I knew — and checked her messages with compulsive regularity. "Might just be your mother-in-law's right about Mr. Todd. Be something funny goin' on anyway."

"How so?"

"Subscriber was Inco of California. Impressive, right? Big outfit of some kind. But the thing is, they had the number exactly one month. September first to October first."

"Cancelled by them or Pac Bell?"

"Them. Paid the setup charge in advance, paid the one month's bill and cancelled at the same time. Not much of a bill, either — "

few dollars over minimum, all on toll calls to Marin."

"Who opened the account and signed Inco's check?"

"Man named John Klinghurst. Mean anything?"

"Not to me."

"Well, Mr. John Klinghurst has himself another phone number listed in his own name. Same billing address as Inco's — twenty-six-eleven Kirkham. That number's still in service."

"Inner Sunset. Residential area."

"Right. All of this say to you what it does to me?"

"Scam of some kind."

"With just one target. Mr. Archie Todd."

"When you get back to the office," I said, "see what you can find out about this John Klinghurst. Call my mother-in-law, ask her if she knows him or has heard the name. And check with Dunbar Asset Management, Todd's financial consultants. If they won't give you any information about his account, talk to his lawyer, Evan Patterson. See what he knows about Todd's financial situation."

"Will do," Tamara said.

We rang off. By then I was through the worst of the cliff-hugging turns and on my way past the old Russian stronghold at Fort Ross. A phrase popped into my head: Trouble ahead, trouble behind, and me somewhere in the middle. I smiled a little, wryly. You could use those words, pretty much verbatim, as an epitaph for a private eye.

13

Gualala is one of several villages strung along the Pacific rim of Sonoma and Mendocino counties, between Fort Ross and Fort Bragg. Some people think the name is Native American, but in fact it's a Spanish phoenetic rendering of Valhalla, the mythological home of heroes fallen in battle. Timber interests working the long spine of mountains to the east built a logging camp there in the 1850's — one of the "doghole ports" used as shipping points for schooners carrying redwood to San Francisco Bay. For over a hundred years much of the Bay Area's lumber supply came from the area.

Its modern evolution began in the early 1960s, when logging went into a big decline. Retirees and wealthy individuals looking for second homes and private retreats began to move in, drawn by some of the most ruggedly unspoiled coastline in the state.

Developers, naturally, weren't far behind. Under close watch by the Coastal Commission, they built a ten-mile-long stretch of environmentally friendly homes on large parcels called Sea Ranch; and farther north, oceanfront property stretching halfway to Point Arena was gobbled up at increasingly higher prices. Gualala, smack in the middle and loaded with old-fashioned seaside charm, flourished for that reason, and because its isolation, generally temperate weather (the area is known as the "Banana Coast"), and scenic attractions made it desirable to artists, writers, and other urban dropouts.

A little of the old charm has been diluted by such growth by-products as minimalls and motels, but for the most part it's still a down-home place. It may not be quite as unspoiled as a few of its "doghole" neighbors, but on the other hand it hasn't gone the way of Mendocino, the best known of the coastal towns fifty miles to the north, and become a cloyingly quaint, tricked-up tourist trap.

It was a quarter of two when I crossed the long bridge spanning the mouth of the Gualala River and entered the town. The weather up here was mostly clear and sunny, but there was a fogbank out at the horizon line and a gusty wind that threatened to drive it inshore before dark. The Banana Coast's mean temperature may be higher than San Francisco's, but it gets just as many year-round smothers of fog.

I pulled into the lot next to the old Gualala Hotel and went in there to ask directions to Port Creek Road. It was at the north end of the village, leading up into the hills. I found it all right, climbed past a school and through a long wooded section. The number 2410 was painted on one of four mailboxes at the foot of a private access lane. The last of the four houses back in there, set on a piece of high ground, was the one I wanted.

It was a small place that had seen better days, built of redwood logs and shakes, with a front deck that looked as though a good wind might knock it down into kindling. Just as ramshackle were an empty carport, a lean-to stuffed with firewood, and a shedlike structure in the trees behind the house. I'd seen woodsmoke coming from the chimneys of two of the other houses; there was none here. Nobody home, evidently.

I left my car on the turnaround where the lane ended and walked up to number 2410. The stairs felt spongy under my feet as I climbed onto the deck. The boards up there were in such bad shape that my weight on them brought creaks and fluttery movement from an ancient chain-supported porch swing. Some place. Aunt Karen wasn't anywhere near as well off as the Hunters. But then, she might be the kind of artist who didn't give a damn about material rewards.

There was no bell so I banged on the door. All that got me was more creaking from the rusty swing. Well? I turned to glance along the lane. The thick growth of pine and fir on the Port Creek Road side cut off any view of the neighboring houses. I faced the door again. Knocked once more, listened, didn't hear anything, and tried the knob. I expected it to be locked; the fact that it wasn't stirred me. I hesitated with my hand on the knob. Better not, I thought, somebody could show up any minute.

Emily, I thought. And opened the door and leaned inside.

Dark in there — curtains open but not much natural light coming through the windows. A faint, pulsing red showed in the fireplace: the last dying embers of a recent fire whose warmth still lingered. I glanced back at the empty lane another time, then went in all the way, leaving the door open so it would be easier to hear the sound of an approaching car.

When my eyes adjusted I could see that the room was maybe twenty feet square. Not much furniture, rag rugs on a bare hardwood floor, a breakfast bar and a pocket-size kitchen to my left. Pieces of stained glass, mounted and suspended from the ceiling, served as wall decoration on both sides of the fireplace. I couldn't tell much about them in the gloom and I wouldn't have been able to judge their quality anyway.

A narrow hallway bisected the wall opposite, next to the kitchen; I went that way, taking in the room. Karen Meineke was not much of a housekeeper. Papers, unemptied ashtrays, unclean dishes, other items littered most surfaces. Woodsmoke, cigarette smoke, fried foods, dust and dampness created a heavy, hanging smell that encouraged mouth breathing. I walked along the hall. A right-angle extension led to one bedroom; another, larger bedroom opened up ahead. The larger one had an unmade brass-frame bed, piles of dirty clothes, and not much else. I backed up and moved into the second bedroom.

Things were neater in there. The bed had been made, the floor was free of personal droppings. The closet door stood open; inside I could see a closed suitcase. The case was small, powder blue, and looked both new and expensive. I squatted and worked the catches. It wasn't locked.

Kid's clothing. Little girl's.

All right, good, I thought as I straightened up. Emily must be staying here, at least. Off somewhere now with Aunt Karen — back eventually.

I searched the closet, the bureau; even got down on all fours and squinted under the bed. Emily's suitcase was the only one, and there was no sign of anything that might belong to her mother. I returned to the other bedroom. Nothing of hers there, either. All the clothing belonged to a woman much larger and far less fashion conscious than Sheila Hunter — jeans, bargain-rack blouses, wool shirts, bulky knit sweaters. That told me something else: Karen Meineke lived here alone. The only item of masculine apparel in the room was a pair of heavy wool socks, of the type that Kerry wore during the winter.

I thought I heard something outside, hurried to the front door for a look. Imagination; the access lane was as deserted as before. Still time to comb through the rest of the place.

Two items of interest turned up in the living room. The first, in the drawer of a table next to an armchair, I didn't like at all — a snub-nosed Smith & Wesson .38, all its chambers full. Loaded gun just lying around like that, with a ten-year-old in the house. Stupid and irresponsible. I stood looking at it for a few seconds. Then I emptied the cylinder, dumped the cartridges into a paper sack of garbage under the kitchen sink, and carried the piece into Karen Meineke's bedroom and hid it on the top shelf of the closet under a jumble of caps and scarves. Let her go hunting for it and wonder how it got there, empty, when she found it.

The second interesting item I found on a shelf in a storage closet — a photograph album with cracked plastic covers. About two-thirds of it was filled, mostly with candid color snapshots. There were half a dozen professional photos, three posed portraits and three wedding pictures. Two of the portraits, judging from the head-and-shoulders poses and the subjects' age and clothing, were high school graduation photos. The young woman in one was unmistakably Sheila Hunter, even though her eyebrows were thicker and her hair dark brown and shag cut. The young woman in the other had a round face, a pouty mouth, the same color hair worn longer. Karen Meineke. The resemblance between her and Sheila Hunter was plain enough, and the third portrait pretty much confirmed the fact that they were sisters. It was of the pair of them, their shoulders touching, their heads turned slightly so that they were smiling at each other. The resemblance was even stronger in that one.

I slid the portraits out to see if anything was written on the backs. No. The three wedding photos were of Karen Meineke and a tall man with a beard and shoulder-length hair; she appeared to be in her early to mid-twenties at the time, as did the man. The backs of two were blank, but the third — a full-length portrait of the bride and groom — bore a notation in a round girlish hand: *Mr. and Mrs. Chas Willis,* and below that, *Yes!*

I took a quick flip through the candid shots. Most were of the two sisters, some with adults who were probably their parents and other family members, ranging from infancy to late teens. The last two dozen or so were of Karen Meineke and her bearded husband; a couple of those had snowcapped mountains in the background. At random I chose four of the sisters together, from girlhood to adulthood. All had tag lines on their backs, the first two in ballpoint pen in a precise hand — their mother's, likely — and the last two in the round, girlish hand.

Lynn's 6th birthday party.

Ellen and Lynn, 4th of July parade.
Me and Ellen, summer '84.
Ellen, sweet 16 and never been kissed — ha!
Me 18 and still a virgin — ha!

Ellen: Sheila Hunter. Lynn: Karen Meineke.

So Aunt Karen's name was also a new identity, no doubt adopted for the same unknown reason. Chas Willis, too? Mr. Meineke? Depended on exactly when the two of them had been married. No clue here as to Jack Hunter's real identity; or if there was, I couldn't pick it out because I'd never seen a photo of him.

I put the album back where I'd found it. I'd been in here long enough; pressing my luck as it was. I checked out front — empty and quiet except for the yattering of jays in the pines — and then stepped onto the porch and shut the door behind me.

I went down and around to have a look at the outbuilding behind the house. It was bigger than a shed, but not by much, with a flat tarpaper roof — the kind of structure that gets put up fast and as cheaply as possible without a building permit. If it had a window, it was on the side opposite where I was. The door was on the back side, and for some reason it had been wedged shut by means of a two-by-four fitted slantwise from

186

the ground to the knob. Busted latch? The length of wood was tightly jammed; I had to kick it loose. The door didn't come open when the two-by-four popped free, so the latch was all right. And not locked. I opened up and stuck my head inside.

Karen Meineke's workshop. Cluttered with tools and sawhorses and pieces of plywood and bars of lead, the walls honeycombed with cubbyholes that contained chunks of colored glass. And not as empty as I'd expected. It jarred me when I saw that the cold, dark room had an occupant and who it was.

Emily Hunter. Sitting hunched on a stool in one shadowy corner, like a bad little girl being punished.

She recognized me, said my name and hopped off the stool. But she didn't move in my direction; she stood very straight, her arms down at her sides — a small, forlorn figure bundled in a fur-collared coat.

"I knew you'd come," she said.

"Are you okay?"

"Oh, yes. Just cold. It's cold in here."

"Come outside into the sun."

We went around to the front of the house. She walked close to me and stayed close when I stopped in a patch of sunlight near the stairs, as if she were afraid I might go away and leave her alone again. She was pale except for splotches of color the cold had put across her cheekbones. Otherwise she seemed all right. No visible marks on her. If there had been, I don't know what I would have done.

She said, "My aunt's not back yet. Good."

"She the one who put you in the shed?"

"Yes."

"How long ago?"

"I don't know. Not long."

"So you wouldn't run away or use the phone."

"Yes."

"Where'd she go?"

"Shopping. She won't take me with her when she goes into town because she's afraid I'll say something to somebody or try to get away."

"How many times has she locked you up?"

"One other time. Yesterday."

I had to work to hide my anger behind a poker face. "She hasn't hit you or anything like that?"

"No. She doesn't like me, but she wouldn't hurt me."

"Why doesn't she like you? She's your real aunt, isn't she?"

Emily nodded. "She hates kids, I guess.

Kids are a pain in the ass, that's what she said."

"She live here alone?"

"Yes. She and Uncle Mike are divorced."

"Uncle Mike. Mike Meineke?"

"Yes."

"How long have they been divorced?"

"I think I was about eight. Two years."

"Where does he live now?"

"I don't know. Up here somewhere, I think. Do you know where my mother is?"

"I was going to ask you. She brought you up here?"

"Yes. On Friday."

"How long did she stay?"

"Just a few minutes. She and Aunt Karen went outside to talk so I couldn't hear them."

"So it was late Friday afternoon when she left. Did she tell you where she was going?"

Nod. "Back home. She was supposed to come pick me up Saturday night or Sunday morning, but she didn't. At first I was glad because I knew you'd come when you got my letter. But now I'm worried. She hasn't called and she doesn't answer the phone. Aunt Karen's called home a dozen times. She's really upset."

So am I, I thought. "Where were you going after she picked you up?"

"Someplace new to live. She wouldn't say where."

"Emily, was anyone with you and your mom when you drove up here?"

"No. Just us."

"And you came in your mother's car?"

"Yes."

"Did she say why she needed to go back home right away?"

"Some things she had to take care of."

"Meet someone? Trevor Smith?"

"I don't think so. She didn't want to see him anymore."

I ran it around inside my head. Some things to take care of. The money kind, maybe; and the loose ends kind. Close out bank accounts, clean out safe-deposit boxes — banks are open on Saturdays now. Make sure there was nothing incriminating or revealing left in the house. Tasks she hadn't had time to do or to finish doing on Friday. Her first priority, or one of the first, had been to stash Emily with her sister, keep her away from me. But what had happened after her return to Greenwood? Why was her car still parked in the garage and where was she? And how did Dale Cooney's death connect with her disappearance, if it did?

Emily asked, "What're we going to do now?"

"Wait for your aunt to get back so I can talk to her."

"About what's making everybody so scared."

"That's right. Do you have any idea what it is?"

"No. Nobody will tell me anything. It must be something really awful if a man wants to kill my mom."

"Did she say his name, even his first name?"

"No."

"Your aunt knows who he is."

"Yes, and I want to know, too."

"She won't talk about it in front of you."

"I know," Emily said. "Will you tell me if you can make her tell you?"

Difficult question. She had a right to know; it involved her parents, her aunt, and it was having an immediate and chaotic effect on her life. Mature for her age, but still a kid, with a kid's emotions, and she had already suffered a devastating blow with the death of her father. "Something really awful" might open wounds that would never heal.

I hedged by saying, "Maybe it's best if you don't know everything, at least not right away."

"That means you won't tell me anything."

"Emily, do you trust me?"

". . . Yes."

"Then believe this. I won't keep anything really important from you, but I have to know all the facts first. That means talking to other people besides your aunt."

"I'm not a baby," she said.

"I know you're not. And I'm not treating you like one. I'm telling you the same thing I'd tell an adult." Which was the truth, and to prove it to her I held her gaze, let her see it in my eyes.

"All right," she said slowly. "But I hate not knowing. I hate being afraid."

"Me, too," I said. "Always."

A jay began squalling in one of the pines. The racket turned my head for a few seconds. When I looked down at Emily again, she said, "Is it okay if I go with you?"

"With me?"

"When you leave. After you talk to Aunt Karen."

It caught me off guard; I didn't have an immediate answer.

"Please? You're going to look for my mother, aren't you? In Greenwood? I don't want to stay here anymore. Aunt Karen . . . she doesn't want me and she makes me more afraid. Please let me go with you."

Christ. What *can* you say?

"Please," she said again.

"I wish I could." Also the truth, gently. "But I can't."

"Why not?"

"You're in your aunt's care. I can't just take you away."

"Even if I say it's what I want?"

"You're a minor, Emily. I'd have to have written permission, and when your aunt finds out who I am she'll never give it. Besides, your mom expects you to be here. Suppose she's on her way right now? She'd be frantic if she found you gone."

"I don't think she's on her way." Now it was her eyes, big and dark and tragic, holding mine. "I don't think she's going to come at all."

Another sound saved me from having to fumble up a response to that. This one was the thrum and whine of an approaching car. I swung around to look along the access lane.

"That's Aunt Karen's van," Emily said.

14

I caught Emily's hand and drew her with me around to the side of the house opposite the carport. I did not want Karen Meineke to see the two of us standing in plain view; it was liable to panic her. We got into heavy tree shadow just before a beat-up yellow Volkswagen van rattled into sight, polluting the air with blackish smoke from a defective exhaust. If the driver noticed my car parked on the turnaround, it didn't alarm her; the van came up the driveway and into the carport without slowing. The noisy engine and the defective pipe combined to produce an explosive farting sound when the ignition was switched off.

The woman who stepped out and came around to open the rear doors weighed at least forty pounds more than she had on her wedding day, a lot of the extra poundage in bulging hips that rolled and wobbled inside a pair of jogger's sweatpants. Her hair was a hennaed red now, long and stringy under a dark-green stocking cap. While she unloaded a couple of grocery bags, her back to the house, I whispered to Emily, "Stay here until I call you." She nodded and I moved out into the open, walked slowly toward the carport.

I was halfway there, adjacent to the stairs again, when Karen Meineke turned and saw me. She had a grocery bag in each arm; she almost dropped one, recovered just in time, and then came up on the balls of her feet and swiveled her head left and right like a trapped animal looking for an escape route. That initial reaction lasted four or five seconds, as long as it took her to realize I was alone and not particularly menacing — empty hands, casual movements. Then she seemed to suck in a breath, gain control of herself. She came forward jerkily to meet me.

"Who are you?" Thin, shaky voice. Deep-sunk eyes wary and hiding things. "What're you doing on my property?"

"Waiting for you, Mrs. Meineke."

"Why? What d'you want?"

"Information."

"About what?"

"You and your sister."

"My — I don't have a sister."

"Sure you do. Ellen. Ellen and Lynn, sisters."

The hidden things crawled into the light of her eyes, and they were the naked shapes of terror. "Jesus," she said in a sick voice, "oh, Jesus, you . . . you're . . ."

"That's right. The detective Ellen told you about."

She backed up a step, and for a second I thought the fear might goad her into flight. That might have happened if the one bag hadn't slipped again, this time free of her clutch. The sound of it splitting on the hard ground seemed to freeze her in place. She glanced down at the scatter of canned goods, cookie packages, a burst quart of milk. When her eyes came up to mine again they had a stunned sheen. Her face was as white as the spilled milk.

"I'm not gonna talk to you," she said.

"You'd better, Lynn. For your own good."

"Karen. My name's Karen. You get out of here and leave me alone. This is my property, you have no right to be here. I don't have to talk to you, you can't make me . . ."

Babbling. I waited until she ran down. Then I said, "What happened ten years ago?"

She shook her head. Shook it again, hard enough to wobble chins and jowls.

"Why did you and your sister change your names?"

"No," she said. "No!"

"Where's Ellen now?"

"I don't . . . how do I know where she is?"

"She went back to Greenwood Friday afternoon," I said. "Why? Who was she planning to see?"

"I don't know what you're talking about. She . . . nobody came here Friday, nobody's been here in weeks — "

"There's no use in lying. I know she was here. I know she brought Emily with her."

"No. Leave me alone." The fear was a living thing in the woman's body; it made her quiver, jerked her legs into motion. She backed up another step, looking down again at the split bag of groceries, then went sideways in a kind of unsteady loop away from me toward the cabin. I let her get to within half a dozen paces of the stairs before I moved over to block her.

"You get out of my way," she said without looking at me. "If you don't leave me alone I'll call the law. You hear me? I'll call the sheriff and have you arrested . . ."

"No you won't. Then I'd have to tell them what I already know about you and Ellen."

"You don't know anything. You can't make trouble for me."

"I know enough," I said. "I'd have to tell them what you did to Emily, too."

"...What?"

"Emily. Locking her up in that studio of yours. No heat, no toilet facilities — that's abuse, Mrs. Meineke. Child abuse and child endangerment."

"You . . . found . . ." She choked on the rest of it. Her face was splotched with red now, as if droplets of blood had been stirred into the milk-white.

"That's right, I found her. And I let her out." I raised my voice. "Emily, you can come over now."

Karen Meineke stared as her niece appeared. Emily stopped beside me, as close as she'd stood before. She didn't say anything; she just looked at the woman with those wide, tragic eyes.

"I never touched her," Karen Meineke said. "I never hurt the kid. You tell him I never laid a hand on you, Emily."

"She already told me," I said.

"I had to put her in the studio. Her mother . . . Oh, shit, I never wanted her here in the first place!"

Emily said, "I don't want to be here. I want to go home." Her small fingers clutched at my coat sleeve. "I want him to take me home, Aunt Karen."

The woman stared at her with cringing amazement. "What's the matter with you? Your mother's coming back for you."

"No, she's not. She'd've been here by now if she was. Please, Aunt Karen?"

"Ellen . . . your mother . . . she's coming, I tell you. She has to. If you're not here, she'll . . . No, you're staying right here with me." Karen Meineke was sweating now; she reached out with her free hand to clutch at the porch railing, as if she might suddenly be feeling dizzy. "God, I wish I'd never . . . I wish . . ."

"Never what?" I said. "Never had a sister? Never done what you did ten years ago?"

"I didn't do anything. It wasn't me, it was them . . . Ellen and that bastard she . . . It wasn't our idea, they talked us into it."

"You and your husband, Charles Willis."

She winced at the name.

"What did they talk you into doing?"

"I can't tell you. I won't."

"I'll find out one way or another. And soon. You know that. You know you can't keep on lying and pretending."

"Damn you, leave me alone! If you don't, I'll — " Hot little flicker in her eyes; she'd had a sudden thought. It straightened her up, gave her the impetus to push past me and start up the stairs.

When she'd gone partway I called, "If you're going after a weapon, say a handgun, I don't think you'll find it where you left it."

The words stopped her. She pivoted, both arms hugging the remaining grocery bag to her chest. "You . . . you were in my house. You broke into my house!"

"Did I? Front door doesn't seem to be locked. Besides, you weren't here — you don't know if I was inside or not."

"Broke in and stole my gun — "

"I'm not a thief," I said. "Misplaced weapons have a way of turning up. Empty, even though you think you've left them lying around loaded."

"You son of a bitch!" She screamed the epithet at me. And lumbered up the rest of the way and banged into the house.

As much to myself as to Emily I said, "It's no use. I'll have to find out some other way."

"Do I *have* to stay here with her?"

"I'm afraid so. There's no other choice."

"For how long?"

"Until your mom comes or I find her first. If she does show up, you tell her to take you straight home. Tell her she can't run and hide anymore, I'll find her wherever she goes."

"She isn't coming back here," Emily said.

Ah, Christ. I had my doubts, too, but I

didn't want her to know it. I said, "You'll be all right here. Your aunt won't lock you up anymore."

Those dark, pained eyes moved over my face; I could almost feel them like a feather touch on my skin. "*You'll* come back, won't you? You won't just leave me here?"

"I'll be back. As soon as I can."

"Promise?"

"Promise."

Eye contact for a few more seconds. Emily broke it, took a couple of hesitant steps away from me — and changed her mind and came back and threw her arms around my waist, hugged me briefly and very hard. Then she ran up the stairs and into the house without looking back.

I felt lousy, standing there alone in the sun. I felt like the world's biggest shit.

All the way into Gualala I beat myself up about leaving Emily to the not very tender mercies of her aunt. But it was the only option, just as I'd told her. If I had taken her with me and Karen Meineke decided to be vengeful, I'd be wide open for a kidnapping charge. And I couldn't keep doing my job if I had a kid to watch out for, could I? Verities, sure, but they didn't make me feel any better about it.

In the village, because my empty stomach was giving me hell, I stopped at a seafood restaurant that looked as though it catered to local trade and made short work of a bowl of clam chowder. Emily had said she thought her uncle still lived somewhere in the area; there was no listing in the local phone book for a Mike Meineke — I'd checked the restaurant's pay-phone copy on the way in — so I asked my waitress if she knew him. No. Same response from the handful of other patrons.

From there I made the rounds of other local businesses. The fourth place I tried was The Fisherman's Bar and Grill, on Highway 1 north of Port Creek Road. The bar was presided over by a big, bearded gent with hair as thick as fur on his arms and hands. When I asked him he if he knew Meineke, he said, "Looking for the man why?"

"Good news for him," I lied. I handed over one of my cards. "I work for an attorney in San Francisco, executor of the estate of one of Mr. Meineke's relatives."

"Left him some money, this relative?"

"A small bequest, yes."

The only customer within earshot, a wizened little guy drinking draft beer, leaned toward us and said, "If it's more than five bucks, you can leave it right here with Hank.

This is where Meineke'll come spend it anyways."

"You know him, then."

"Sure, we know him," Hank said. He winked at the customer. "Mike's been known to take a drink now and then."

"That's a fact," the little guy agreed. "If he has to knock you down to get hold of the bottle."

The two of them thought that was pretty funny. I didn't, particularly, but I laughed with them so they'd be inclined to answer my next question.

"Where can I find him?"

"Well, if he's sober," Hank said, "he'll be up at the Wilkerson property. Hollywood people, the Wilkersons, come up here two weeks out of the year. Must be nice to be rich."

"What does Meineke do there?"

"Lives there, takes care of the place."

"Far from here?"

"Six, seven miles. Up north of Anchor Bay."

"I'd appreciate directions."

He asked shrewdly, "Get you something to drink first?"

I ordered a beer I didn't want, bought a refill for the little guy and a shot of bourbon for Hank. That made the three of us drinking buddies and got me directions explicit enough for a backward child to follow.

15

Anchor Bay was a few miles above Gualala, and the winding stretch of Highway 1 north of there was a pretty one — thickly wooded slopes to the east, the ocean close on the west and visible in snatches through more pine woods running along the cliff tops. Wisps of fog threaded the blue sky now; but the wind had slacked off and the offshore bank was moving slowly. The lowering sun had lost some of its brightness, so that its rays among the trees had a pale, filtered look.

At the six-mile point on the odometer I began scouting for the landmarks I'd been given. When the last of them appeared near the top of a rise — somebody's mailbox built large to resemble a birdhouse — I slowed down. The Wilkerson driveway was just beyond the crest, half hidden by trees and undergrowth. I almost missed it, braked just in time to make the turn ahead of an on-coming logging truck.

Some nice piece of oceanfront property lay ahead of me, spread out behind a gated fence. At least two wooded acres, with an ultra-modern wood-and-stone house squatting at the edge of the cliff and a couple of outbuildings in the trees closer to the highway. The security gates were open — I seemed to be lucky in that respect lately. The reason here was a stakebed truck parked midway along the drive, its bed mounded with dry brush and tree branches. A man dressed in overalls was clearing out more dead wood under the pines nearby.

I drove on through and stopped behind the truck. The man had straightened and was coming my way by then, dragging a six-foot limb in one gloved hand. I got out, walked around to meet him.

"Afternoon," I said. "I'm looking for — "

"Wilkersons ain't here. Not expected, either."

He was thirty-five or so, all bone and gristle. Gray stubble flecked hollow cheeks and a weak chin. Broken capillaries made a tracery of red and blue lines across nose and cheekbones; the whites of his eyes had blood in them, like the albumin of a fertilized egg. You had to look close to see that he was the same man in the wedding photo, and not because he was lacking the beard and his hair was cut short. Even then I couldn't be a hundred percent positive.

"Your name Meineke? Mike Meineke?"

"Why? I don't know you and I'm not buying anything."

"I'm not selling anything. I'm here about your sister-in-law."

"Who you talking about?"

"Sheila Hunter. Or I should say Ellen. Lynn's sister. Their real names, right, Mr. Willis?"

He stared at me. The bloodshot eyes showed fear now, but it was not the consuming terror I'd seen in Emily's mother and aunt; it was a shadow, a wraith, of something that had grown weak and shriveled with age.

"So it's finally happened," he said. "All along I figured it would someday. A man like Cotter never gives up, no matter how long it takes."

I let the name slide by for the moment. "Ten years," I said.

"Yeah. Almost eleven." His mouth worked as if all his spit had dried up. "What happens now?"

"To Ellen?"

"Her, Pete, Lynn. Me."

"Pete. Ellen's husband."

"Who the hell else?"

"He's dead. Two weeks now."

"Jesus," Meineke said. "Cotter do it? You?"

"No, he died in a head-on collision with a drunk driver."

That confused him. He shook his head.

I said, "Nobody told you? Your ex-wife knows."

"Her. We ain't said a word to each other in two years."

"Tell me about Ellen and Pete."

"Tell you what? If you work for Cotter — "

"I don't work for Cotter. I don't know Cotter."

"Listen," Meineke said, and shook his head again, and worked his dry mouth. "Just who the hell are you?"

"A private detective. Working for Jack Hunter's insurance company. And for his daughter."

"Emily? She's a kid. That don't make sense."

"You make sense for me, I'll do the same for you."

"I don't have to talk to you. You're not from Cotter, you said you don't even know him."

"Talk to me or to the police. Your choice."

"Police? Oh, no, you don't. I didn't do nothing wrong. Lynn and me, we had nothing to do with stealing those bonds — " He broke off, his gaze sliding away from mine.

"What bonds, Mike?"

"No," he said.

"Pete and Ellen stole them, right?"

"No."

"And you knew about it, maybe shared in the profits — "

"No."

"Either way, you're an accessory to a felony. You can go to prison, minimum of five years, if I report it to the authorities."

That was more bluff than not. If theft was the only serious crime here, it had happened long enough ago for the statute of limitations to have run out. If Meineke knew that —

But he didn't know it. He still wasn't meeting my eyes and there was a slump to his body now, a loosening of his facial muscles — all signs of defeat in a man. He'd talk to me. All I had to do was give him back a little hope.

"I don't want to make trouble for you, Mike. Facts are what I'm after. Give them to me and I'm out of your life as fast as I came into it."

He ran a gloved hand over his face; I

could hear the scraping of cloth on beard stubble. His eyes flicked up. "No cops?"

"No cops."

"All right. What the hell. But I need a drink first. Christ, I need one bad."

He put his back to me and shambled down the driveway. I followed him to the nearest of the outbuildings, a small, square cabin made of redwood logs and shakes that could not have contained more than two rooms. I went all the way into the doorway to make sure a drink was all he was after. A full pint of cheap bourbon stood on a table next to a bunk bed; he snagged it and took a long pull, then put the cap back on and came outside with it.

He didn't say anything to me or even look at me. He walked around the side of the cabin, onto a beaten path that cut through the trees to the cliff's edge. A bench had been anchored there facing the ocean; Meineke sat down on it and slugged again from the bottle. It seemed colder out there, in the pale sun with the vanguards of mist curling in overhead. I buried my hands in my coat pockets, went around and stood on the other side of the bench. From there you could look down a hundred feet of eroded rock wall to a whitewater cover where waves broke over offshore rocks and kelp beds.

209

The big main house was about fifty yards away and partially screened by pines. If you sat with your back to it, I thought, as Meineke was sitting, you'd have a sense of what it was like to be all alone on the edge of the world.

"Come out here every chance I get," he said. "Ocean's about all I got left now. Ocean and booze."

I had nothing to say to that.

"Fucking money never bought me anything but grief. Lynn and me, we were happy in Colorado before it happened. We didn't have a pot but we had each other. We had something."

"The bonds belonged to Cotter?" I asked.

"Yeah. Philip fucking Cotter."

"Bearer bonds?"

"That's what Pete said. Some cash, too."

"How much altogether?"

"Couple of hundred thousand, Pete told us. Lying bastard. Had to be more than that, the way those two lived down in Greenwood. A hell of a lot more."

"Why would he lie to you?"

"Why you think? So we wouldn't ask for more than him and Ellen were offering."

"How much was that?"

"Fifty thousand. Seemed like a fortune at the time." Another slug at the bottle. "Man,

I wish I'd told 'em to take their fifty grand and shove it."

"Why'd they give you that much?"

"So we'd move, change our names, start a new life like they were doing. So Cotter wouldn't come after Lynn and me, try to find them through us. He knew where we lived. No question he'd've made us pay, too."

"What was Ellen's relationship with Cotter?"

"Married to him."

"Where was this? Colorado?"

"Illinois. Billington, little town near Chicago."

"What did Cotter do there?"

"Owned a company manufactured some kind of appliance — toasters, something like that. Goddamn laundry is what it was."

"Laundry? You mean money laundering?"

"Yeah."

"Mob-connected, then, this Cotter."

"Not big time, but yeah, connected."

"The stolen bonds and cash — his or the mob's?"

"Cotter's," Meineke said. "Jesus, if it'd belonged to the fucking Mafia, Pete and Ellen would never've touched it. Bad enough having a sick, ruthless son of a bitch like Cotter looking for us."

"Sick?"

"Got his kicks hurting people. I mean hurting 'em with his hands."

"Did he hurt Ellen?"

"Oh, yeah. Some of the things she told Lynn . . . make you puke." Meineke grimaced, gulped bourbon. "One of his favorite tricks, if she did something he didn't like, he'd take a ballpeen hammer and smack her on both elbows until she passed out from the pain."

"Crazybone," I said.

"Yeah. Nothing hurts worse than getting hit there."

I looked away from him, down at the rocks below. One of the larger ones offshore had been sea-sculpted into a shape that resembled a castle on a mount; when the surf broke over it, the white spume gave it a sparkling, immaculate quality. Illusion. Bare black stone was all it was, and beneath the surface dark things clung to it and it was coated with slime.

Pretty soon I said, "How long was Ellen married to him?"

"Two years. Met him when he went to Cincinnati on a business trip."

"That where she and Lynn are from, Cincinnati?"

"Yeah. Lynn's older, she moved away a

couple of years before and ended up in Boulder."

"Why didn't Ellen divorce Cotter when she found out what he was?"

"Didn't have no money of her own — he made her sign one of those prenuptial agreements. And he told her he'd kill her if she tried to leave him."

"Too scared to file for divorce, but not too scared to steal from him and then go on the run. How does that add up?"

"Wasn't her idea. Pete talked her into it."

"Where does he fit in?"

"Screwing him back then," Meineke said. "Fell in love with him, she said, couldn't help herself. At least he treated her decent."

"What else was he? What was his work?"

"CPA. One of Cotter's. That's how she met him."

"On the money-laundering end of the business?"

"Not according to Pete."

"What was his last name?"

"Stoddard. Pete Stoddard. Orphan, so *he* didn't have a family to worry about and buy off."

"All right. How'd the two of them get hold of the bonds?"

"Cotter had a safe at home," Meineke said. "He was the only one knew the combination, but Ellen found it out somehow. Or Pete did. Never too clear about that."

"Doesn't matter. Where'd they go to cash the bonds?"

"New York someplace. Pete had that part of it figured out."

One or more discount brokerage firms, probably. Quick sale on all or most of the bonds. Take the money to different brokers or money management firms, have it invested in a stock portfolio under the new Hunter name; and keep the stolen cash to buy off her relatives and for traveling expenses. Then, as time passed, draw out just as much of the stock dividends as needed and reinvest the rest. And pretty soon you'd be well off enough to afford a four-hundred-thousand-dollar house and a free and easy lifestyle in a place like Greenwood. It was just the kind of plan a CPA with enough guts, patience, and gambler's instincts would come up with.

I said, "And when they were done in New York, they came to see you and Lynn in Colorado."

"Just showed up in Boulder one night. Told us what they'd done, laid out their offer." Meineke belched sourly and wagged his head. "I was a musician in those days. Called myself one anyway. Shit. Played lousy guitar for a lousy band, didn't make much bread. Lynn was supporting us, waitressing in a cafe."

"So the offer looked plenty good to you."

"Good? Man, fifty thousand in cash was more than we ever hoped to see in one lump. Plus, they said they'd pay all our expenses for a year. We didn't have much time to think it over. They'd picked a time when Cotter was away on a trip to hit the safe and take off. Five days until he was due back and they'd already used up three. Maybe if we'd had more time we'd've seen what a goddamn trap it was and turned 'em down." He drank. "Yeah, maybe. But probably not."

"Four of you leave Boulder together?"

"Yeah. In the car Pete'd bought for them in New York — he went there a couple of times before they stole the bonds, setting things up. We just left our old heap behind."

"Headed where?"

"No place in particular, that was part of the plan. Picked a direction and drove until we got to a place none of us'd ever been before, turned out to be Spokane. We were there about three months. Pete had a way to get birth certificates, real ones, something to do with infants who died of natural causes. That's how him and Ellen got their new names, how Lynn and me ended up with

ours. Mike Meineke, a dead baby's name."
He drank, shuddered, drank again. "Christ,
you don't know what it's like. Living with a
dead baby's name for ten years."

I didn't want to know what it was like; I
steered him off the subject. "And once you
had the birth certificates, then you applied
for social security cards and driver's licenses
to cement the new identities."

"Yeah."

"Where'd you go from Spokane?"

"Salt Lake City. Pete and Ellen got married there. Couple of other cities, and then
Albuquerque. That's where the four of us
split up. Pete gave me and Lynn the fifty
thousand cash — that was the deal, full
amount in cash when we quit traveling together. Gave us the car, too. They took a
plane to Phoenix, got a place, let us know
the address. Then we drove out here."

"How long did they stay in Phoenix?"

"Three, four months. Too hot in the summer, so they moved to San Diego for a
while. Didn't like it there and headed north,
wound up in Greenwood. Who knows why
they stuck there? The kid, maybe. Emily.
Ellen had her in Greenwood. Already
knocked up when they left Phoenix."

"What about you and Lynn?"

"First place we went was Mendocino.

She'd heard about it, big artist's colony, she figured we'd both fit in, get a new start. Yeah, sure. You ever see her stained glass? Lousy. Lousy artist, lousy musician." Slug. "Lousy," he said.

"How long were you there?"

"Four lousy years. Up on the Oregon coast for a while. Portland. Back to Mendocino and then down here." Meineke swallowed bourbon, wiped his mouth with the back of one hand. The bottle was almost empty. He'd guzzled close to a pint in under fifteen minutes, but color in his sunken cheeks was the only visible effect. His voice was a steady, emotionless monotone, the voice of a hollow man. "Should've been the good life," he said. "Was for a while, I guess, but we went through the fifty thousand like shit through a goose. Food, liquor, rent, new car, all kinds of crap we didn't need. Didn't work much, either of us — no money coming in. Broke by the time we quit Mendocino the first time. Lived hand to mouth after that. And Pete and Ellen down there in Greenwood with their fancy house, fancy lifestyle. We drove down one time, didn't tell 'em we were coming, and they were pissed. Didn't want us to see how much they really had. Bastards lied about how much they got from Cotter, all right.

Owed us better for sticking with 'em, that's what Lynn said. Never've gotten away with it if we hadn't disappeared along with 'em."

He was right about that, I thought. Still, the planning had been good, careful, and they'd had luck on their side. Statistics, too: fifty thousand people disappear every year in this country, a large percentage without a trace. The police, with all their resources, can't find them; private investigators, with all our resources, can't find them. The irony was, if any outfit could have tracked the four down, it was organized crime with all *their* resources. But Pete and Ellen hadn't ripped off the mob. Cotter's bonds, Cotter's cash, and Cotter was at most a low-level under-boss, more likely a private-sector recruit used strictly for the money laundering. They might've given him some help in the beginning, as a favor, but it would not have involved much manpower or funds and it would have had a time limit. Organized crime's *capos* can't be bothered in the long run with personal problems or personal vendettas.

I asked Meineke, "How much more money did Pete and Ellen give you?"

"Not enough. Never enough. Christ, I hate to beg. Lynn don't mind, she'll lick your ass for fifty bucks. Licked their asses often enough, that's for sure."

"That why the two of you split up?"

"One of the reasons. Nothing left between us, we weren't even screwing any more after she got so goddamn fat. Couldn't stand living with her anymore. Caretaker job came up — not this one, another one up in Elk — I took it and walked. Lynn, she kept right on licking their asses. But not me, not anymore."

One last pull and the bottle was empty. He held it up, peering at it or through it. I thought he might heave it over the cliff to shatter on the rocks below, but he didn't; he tucked it carefully into his coat pocket. Maybe because the ocean was one of the two things he had left, as he'd said, and he did not want to befoul it with the remains of the other thing.

I said, "Ellen's been up to see Lynn. She brought your niece with her."

"Yeah?"

"You didn't know that?"

"How would I know? Told you, I don't have nothing to do with any of 'em anymore."

"She left Emily with Lynn. Supposed to come back and get her, but she hasn't shown up. That's why I'm here."

"Running again? Ellen?"

"Looks that way."

"Why? You don't work for Cotter, you said."

"It's a long story. You care enough to want to hear it?"

"No. Fuck her and Lynn both."

"Your niece, too? She's ten years old, Meineke."

"Their kid, ain't she?"

I stepped away from the bench. The wind had kicked up and the incoming fog had taken away most of the sunlight; my hands were cold even inside the coat pockets. "Okay, we're finished," I said.

He swiveled his head to look at me. His eyes had a ravished look. "No cops, huh, like you said?"

"No cops." I started away.

"Hey," he said, and I stopped again. "What about Cotter? You think he'll find us someday? Any of us?"

"Could be he's dead by now."

"Could be," Meineke said, but he didn't believe it.

"Does it matter much if he does?"

No answer. I left him sitting there staring out to sea, all alone with Philip Cotter and the rest of his demons.

16

So now I had the full story. Or did I?

None of what Meineke had told me explained Sheila Hunter's sudden disappearance, unless the sadistic Philip Cotter had finally found her after ten long years and that was too much coincidence to credit. The stolen bearer bonds and the rest of the scam didn't explain Dale Cooney's death, either. There was more going on here, whether it was related to the actions of four morally bankrupt individuals a decade ago or to something in the present lives of the two principal players. My best guess was the latter. The Hunters might have been a close-knit unit in the beginning, when they were on the run with their ill-gotten gains, but time and the ever-present fear of being caught had pulled them apart. Each had taken lovers, and that could have led to deadly secrets of a different kind.

Emily was on my mind again as I drove back down the coast. Innocent caught in the middle. Father dead, mother missing, unwanted by either unstable aunt or alcoholic uncle. I doubted I could ever bring myself to tell her the meaning of crazybone, or the fact that she was the illegitimate daughter of a bigamous mother, or any of the other ugly things I'd just learned.

I kept thinking of her waiting with Karen Meineke. Of how unpredictable and irrational people could be when they were teetering on the edge of panic. She wouldn't harm Emily, wouldn't lock her up again in that cold shed — not under normal circumstances she wouldn't. But these weren't normal circumstances, and besides, I didn't really know the woman at all. How could you be sure of what a stranger would or wouldn't do, given the wrong tick or enough provocation?

I shouldn't have left that .38 there, I thought. She'll comb the house for it, and even if she doesn't find the cartridges in the garbage sack, she can always go out and buy more . . .

Coming into the outskirts of Gualala now. The turnoff for Port Creek Road was just up ahead. When I spotted it I slowed and made the turn without any hesitation. Karen

Meineke's mental state and that frigging gun. A question I'd neglected to ask Emily, too. But those weren't the real reasons I was going back there. The real reason was Emily and the fact that I could not come to terms with abandoning her as I had. To hell with the strict letter of the law and the risk to me; leaving a child alone in the charge of an unstable relative was flat-out wrong.

The first thing I saw when I reached the end of the access lane was that the carport was empty, the VW van nowhere in sight. It put a knot like a fist under my breastbone. I barreled up the driveway, jammed on the brakes, and came out running.

I was on the stairs when I heard the house door open. I slowed then, looking up, as light footfalls sounded on the deck above. Emily. She appeared and stood looking down at me, brushing her hair out of her eyes, smiling a little tentatively.

The knot loosening, I went up the rest of the way. She seemed all right, the same as before except that there was animation in her face, relief in her smile.

"You came back," she said.

"Where's your aunt?"

"She's gone."

"Gone where?"

"I don't know. She packed some of her

clothes and some money she had in a jar and went away."

"Just left you here by yourself."

"She said she wasn't coming back and I should wait here until Mom comes."

These people — damn these selfish people! "How long has she been gone?"

"A while. Not too long after you left. I'm glad she didn't try to make me go with her."

"So am I."

"I knew you'd come," she said again. "I don't know how, I just knew like before."

"I shouldn't've left you in the first place."

"I can go with you now, can't I? Now that Aunt Karen isn't coming back?"

"Well, you can't stay here by yourself, no matter what she told you."

"I'd like to go home."

"I know you would. I'll take you if that's where your mother is. But you can't stay there alone, either."

"Then where will I stay?"

"I can't answer that yet. Someplace safe. You'll have to trust me, Emily."

"I trust you."

Child's mouth to God's ear. I said, "Okay. Let's go in and get your things together."

While she went after her coat and suitcase I took a quick look around. Karen Meineke's bedroom was in an even worse state of disarray than before, drawers pulled out, more clothing and empty hangers on the floor. The .38 was no longer hidden on the closet shelf. In both the front room and kitchen I hunted for a note, anything the woman might have left for her sister. Nothing. Getting away from here, fast, was all she'd cared about. Maybe later, when she was holed up somewhere and the grip of panic had eased, she might try to reestablish contact. Just as likely, she wouldn't. I had only contempt for her whatever her intentions. The important thing was, she was all through putting her niece in harm's way.

On the back of a business card I wrote "Contact me about Emily's whereabouts." I cleared a space on the breakfast bar, propped the card there against a glass. For good measure I laid another card, printed side up, next to it. If Karen Meineke did decide to come home, or if her sister showed up, maybe I'd get a call. But I'd be damn surprised if I did.

On the way to the car I asked Emily the question I'd neglected to ask earlier. "Do you have keys to your house? For the front door and the alarm system?"

"No, not anymore. Mom took them away when she found out I talked to you."

"Some people hide spare keys in case they

lose the ones they carry. You know, in the garage or under pots, places like that."

"We never did."

"Did she keep a spare house key in her studio?"

"I don't think so. I never saw one there."

"What about friends who might have one?"

"We don't have many friends," Emily said. "Why are you asking about keys?"

"If your mom's not home, the house will be locked and the alarm system turned on."

"But you said I couldn't stay there alone . . . Oh. You want to go in and look around."

"Would you mind?"

"No. I just want to find her."

We were both silent until we rolled down through the woods to the intersection with Highway 1. Then Emily said in a small, thin voice, "Something bad's happened to her." It wasn't a question.

I had no response that didn't sound phony or fatuous.

"I think she's dead," Emily said. "I think the man she was afraid of killed her."

Smart — too smart for her own good. It was possible Sheila Hunter was dead, all right, though not by the hand or order of Philip Cotter. But it was equally possible she had decided to abandon her daughter, just

226

as her sister had, to go on the run alone or with somebody else. The second explanation would be almost as much of a hammerblow to Emily's fragile young psyche as the first.

Get her off this tack, for God's sake, I thought. I said, "Emily, we just don't know what the situation is. It's easy to imagine the worst, but it doesn't have to be that way. You know the phrase 'Keep the faith'?" Fatuous as hell, but it was the best I could do.

"Yes."

"Do that, then. Think good thoughts."

"All right." But her voice was listless.

After a little time I asked, "Do you know a lady named Dale Cooney, Mrs. Frank Cooney?"

"I don't think so."

"Don't ever remember hearing the name?"

"No."

"How about a Mr. Lukash — Doc Lukash."

"He's our dentist."

"A friend of your mom's, too?"

"No, just our dentist."

"Did he ever come to your house?"

"Dentists don't make house calls," she said seriously.

"That's right, they don't. Tell me about Trevor Smith."

"I don't know very much about him."

"He came to see your mom last Thursday night, didn't he?"

"Yes. She was really upset that night."

"She'd already told you by then that you were going away?"

"That morning. Mr. Smith made her more upset, but I don't know why. Mom locked me in my room. She didn't want me to hear what they were saying."

Not a word about her mother smacking her. No teller of tales, this little girl. The value of privacy was one good lesson she'd learned from her parents.

"Could you hear anything they said?"

"No. They were in the living room and my room's in the back."

"So they didn't raise their voices, make any noise?"

"No."

"Did your mom say anything about Smith after he left?"

"No."

"But she was still upset?"

"A little calmer, I guess."

"Did anyone else come to the house before you left on Friday?"

"No."

"Anyone call?"

"There was one call, but I don't know

who it was. Mom made me go in my room again."

"Did the call upset her?"

"No."

"Make her happy, relieved, anything like that?"

"No. She was the same afterward."

We were out of Gualala now, heading down Highway 1 through the northern reaches of Sea Ranch. The fog was in and the afternoon had darkened perceptibly under its heavy gray pall. Almost five by the dashboard clock. Eight or so by the time we reached San Francisco, and then what?

I hauled up the mobile phone, punched out Emily's home number from memory. A dozen rings, no answer. Emily was watching me; I could feel the weight of her eyes. She knew what number I was calling. *Something bad's happened to her. I think she's dead.* I held on to the receiver, looking straight ahead, trying to think through the mental echoes of Emily's voice. Going on nine o'clock before I could get her to Greenwood — pretty late to be showing up on somebody's doorsteps. *We don't have many friends.* But there had to be somebody . . . the family of one of her classmates?

"Emily, who's your best friend at school?"

"I don't have a best friend."

"No girlfriends? No one from the riding academy?"

"Well, there's Tracy Dellman, I guess."

"Tracy Dellman. Do you think her folks might let you stay with them for a few days?"

"I don't know. I've never stayed there before."

"What's Tracy's phone number?"

"We don't talk much on the phone."

"Where does she live?"

"Poplar Avenue. Number two-fifty, I think."

I called directory assistance for the Greenwood area. No listing for a Dellman family on Poplar Avenue. Which meant I'd have to show up at their home at nine P.M., a stranger with a little girl in tow. Explanations, fuss . . . the prospect left me cold. There had to be somebody else . . .

"You know Mrs. Purcell, don't you?" I asked. "The lady who runs the art gallery?"

"Not very well."

"Do you like her? Does she like you?"

"I guess so. Do you want me to stay with her?"

"If you'd be comfortable there."

"I wouldn't," Emily said. Then she said, "Are you married?"

". . . Married?"

"You are, aren't you? You wear a wedding ring."

"Yes, I'm married. Emily . . ."

"Then wouldn't it be all right if I stayed with you?"

"I'm not sure that's a good idea."

"Why not? Doesn't your wife like kids?"

"Sure she does. But she has a job, she's even busier than I am . . ."

"I don't mean for a long time," Emily said. "Just for tonight. Wouldn't that be okay? I don't want to go anywhere else tonight. I don't want to be alone with somebody else."

I knew what she meant and I could not think of a way to say no; couldn't quite bring myself to look at her. I stared out at the road and the mist curling and uncurling in the headlights. Time went by, what seemed like a lot of it.

"It's all right if you don't want me," Emily said. "I understand."

Goddamn it, I thought. I said gruffly, "Just for tonight. And don't ever think you're not wanted. Anybody who wouldn't want a nice young lady like you around ought to have his head examined."

"Thank you," she said.

That mist out there was getting thicker. I had to rub my eyes and squint to see the damn road.

I called the condo, didn't get any answer,

231

and then called Bates and Carpenter. Kerry wasn't there, either; her secretary said she'd gone out for drinks with a client. I waited a while and tried the condo again. Buzz, buzz, buzz.

Emily had been quiet for some time. I glanced over at her. For most of the ride she'd sat primly with her hands in her lap; now she was curled up on the seat, had done it so quietly I hadn't even noticed, and was asleep with her head pillowed on one arm against the door. Poor kid; she probably hadn't slept much the past few nights. She looked very small and fragile and vulnerable, and I felt a fresh cut of anger at what her family had done to her. Maybe I was a fool for taking on the role of her protector, but she needed somebody to look out for her, somebody to put her welfare first for a change. Why not me? I knew what it was like to be alone, all right; I'd been alone a lot of years before Kerry came into my life.

I tried the condo number a third time from Jenner, a fourth when I picked up Highway 101 north of Santa Rosa, a fifth waiting to pay the toll on the Golden Gate Bridge. Still no Kerry. Oh, babe, I thought after the last call, just wait until you see what papa's bringing home for you this time.

Kerry beat us to Diamond Heights by about three minutes; she still had her coat on when I walked in with Emily. She couldn't help but be surprised, but you'd have to know her as well as I do to tell it. Poise is one of her best qualities, and compassion is another. She did a better job of making the kid feel at home than I could have: introduced her to Shameless, showed her the guest room, fixed her a sandwich even though Emily said she wasn't hungry and stood over her until she finished most of it, and then got her settled in the living room with the cat on her lap.

My turn, then. In our bedroom with the door shut she said, "All right, explain." She didn't sound upset.

I explained. In detail.

"You did the right thing," she said. "You couldn't just leave her up there alone — my God, no. Or take her to Greenwood and drag her around until you found somebody to care for her."

"It's just for tonight. Tomorrow I'll talk to the Purcell woman — "

"No you won't," Kerry said. "Emily can stay here as long as she needs to. I'll take tomorrow off so she won't have to be alone. I

don't have anything pressing on the calendar."

"You sure you don't mind?"

"I'm sure."

"Couple of mush-hearts, huh?"

"Never mind that," she said. "You just
find out what happened to her mother."

17

Tuesday morning, early: a cold, gray day, fog and low-hanging clouds staining the rustic elegance of Greenwood with a gloomy brush. And nothing had changed on the Hunter property — gates open, house windows blinded, doors locked, alarm system activated, Sheila Hunter's Audi parked in the garage.

Being there again depressed me. It was more than the sameness, the air of permanent abandonment; it was a feeling of hopelessness based on the truths I'd learned yesterday. Dream house and gracious lifestyle built on a foundation of theft, lies, and deceit. A home that was no longer a home to Emily. The only one she'd ever known and now lost to her forever, no matter what had happened to her mother, because her life was irrevocably damaged. It made me all the more determined to find

Sheila Hunter, put an end to that part of the child's anguish as quickly as possible.

The question was how.

Something in the house might give me an idea of where she'd gone and why; my best option right now, or it would be if I could get past that alarm system and inside. Frustrating that the thing was turned on . . .

Well, there *was* a way to shut it off, neutralize it. Sure there was, if I could set it up. Risky, but not very, and probably expensive, and if it worked out it would allow me to break-and-enter just like Samuel Leatherman.

I drove back to Greenwood Road and into a supermarket parking lot; better to make my call from there than hang around the Hunter property. The first name in my address book was the one I wanted: George Agonistes. I tapped out his combination home and office number. His wife, who doubled as his assistant, answered; George wasn't home, but she knew me, and when I told her I had a job for him she gave me his pager number. I called it and then sat back to wait.

Agonistes was in the same business, but rivals we weren't. His caseload was almost exclusively high-tech: electronic surveillance, debugging services, industrial espionage, that sort of thing. He could have served as the model for the Gene Hackman character in *The Conversation*, except that he had four kids as well as his long-suffering wife, two of them in college and one who kept getting busted for drug use; he was a workaholic because he always needed money. To hear him tell it anyway. He was a good guy for the most part — we'd done some mutual back-scratching over the years, always on a monetary basis — but a little of him went a long way. His two middle names were Poormouth and Cheap.

It took fifteen minutes for him to respond to the page. We exchanged the usual amenities and friendly insults, after which he said, "I suppose you need a favor. I never hear from you otherwise."

"That goes both ways, George."

"Well, you know how busy I am."

"Sure. Don't worry, I'm ready and willing to pay for what I want."

"The magic word. You now have my full attention."

"Simple job, won't take up much of your time. I've got a place that has an armed alarm system and I need to get inside without setting it off. That's it."

"Uh-huh. Sounds like another illegal trespass, like the last job I did for you."

"I'm not after bugs this time. And you don't have to enter the premises with me. Or even stick around after the system is disarmed."

"Uh-huh," he said again. "I'm in the sensitive end of the business, remember? I get caught screwing around with alarm systems, I could lose my rep if not my license. I got mouths to feed, college tuitions to pay for, bills up the yang."

The usual Agonistes lament. I countered it by saying, "Saint George. Never done anything illegal in his stellar career, never even once bent the rules."

"Screw you," he said, but without heat.

"Come on, I'm not asking much here. And I've got a good reason or I wouldn't bother you in the first place."

"You and everybody else that wants something."

"Ought to be a piece of cake for a man with your talents. You've forgotten more about electronics than most so-called experts will ever learn. If the Watergate boys had had you along, they'd never have gotten caught."

"I don't roll over for flattery, pal."

"Right. For money, only money."

"We're all whores to one degree or another. What kind of alarm system?"

"M.A.S."

"Madsen, eh? Not the best, not the worst. What type?"

"I don't know from types. Digital key pad outside, probably another one inside. Pretty standard, I'd say."

"Cameras or motion sensors?"

"I doubt it. Looks like doors and windows only."

"What kind of building?"

"Private house."

"Where?"

"Greenwood."

"Uh-oh. High-risk turf."

"Not a problem," I said. "The neighborhood's not ultra-exclusive and the property's secluded. Nobody'll see you working, nobody'll show up to squawk."

"Except possibly the owners."

"Guaranteed that won't happen. You can do it, can't you?"

"Oh, I can do it."

"Piece of cake, right? How much?"

"Well . . . five hundred?"

"Jesus, George, I'm not asking you to get me into City Hall. Besides, I think I'm likely to end up paying for this out of my own pocket."

"No way to lay it off on your client?"

"I doubt it."

"You wouldn't be b.s.ing me, would you?"

"Have I ever? I'm a poor working stiff, same as you."

"Oh, all right," Agonistes said. "Make it two-fifty. That's my bottom line."

"Fair enough."

"For you, maybe. When d'you want the job done?"

"Soon as possible. Some urgency here, George."

"You couldn't wait until tomorrow?"

"I could if I have to, but it won't make me happy."

He let me hear an elaborate sigh. "I'm on a job right now, in the city, and I can't leave until it's finished. Looks like most of the day. I couldn't get down to Greenwood much before five."

"Five's okay with me."

"Meet where?"

"There's a library on the main drag, middle of town. I'll be waiting in the parking lot."

"Bring your checkbook," Agonistes said. Then he said, "Better yet, make it cash," and rang off before I could put up an argument.

Kerry said, "She's still asleep. I just looked in on her."

"Poor kid must be exhausted."

"Yes, and she feels safe here. She's really taken with you, you know."

"Taken?"

"Savior, protector, father figure all wrapped together."

"Grandfather figure is more like it."

"Don't put yourself down. She loved her father, but I doubt he was ever really there for her. You were when she needed somebody the most."

"As long as she doesn't put too much faith in me."

"She knows how bad the situation is," Kerry said, "even if she doesn't know what it's all about. The important thing is, she trusts you."

"Trusts you, too."

"Not completely, but I hope she will. How do things look down there?"

"The same — not good. But I'm trying to be optimistic. It's going to be a long day."

"You do what you have to. I'll take care of Emily."

"It may not be the only long day, you know."

"Understood."

"I mean, this thing could — "

"I *know*. I thought we settled all that last night."

"Yeah, but if it gets to be a burden on you — "

"I've put up with you for ten years," she said. "That means I can put up with anything. Don't worry about me and don't worry about Emily."

Tamara said, "Man, that's some caper those people pulled off. They had balls, you got to give 'em that."

"And plenty of luck. But they paid a damn heavy price."

"Lot of sleepless nights in ten years, I'll bet. No wonder Mrs. Hunter didn't want a detective messing around in her life, dredging up the past and blowing her cover. You think crazybone Cotter's still hunting her?"

"She thinks he is, that's the point. Either that or she's afraid the blown cover will stir up his desire for revenge, bring him after her again. Her sister's just as panicky. Two of them feeding each other's paranoia."

" 'The guilty flee where no man pursueth.' "

"More than likely," I agreed.

"Man must really be some kind of monster. Messed up her head so bad she never got over it."

I agreed with that, too. Then I said, "See what you can find out about Philip Cotter

— fill in the missing pieces."

"Right. So what about Mrs. Hunter? Running again, by herself or with somebody? Dumped the kid on her sister and just took off?"

"Best-case scenario."

"Uh-huh. Golf pro mixed up in it, maybe?"

"If he is, he's not running with her. Not yet, anyhow. Still on the job at Emerald Hills; I talked to him before I called you. He says he hasn't heard from Sheila Hunter since midday Friday."

"You believe him?"

"At this point I don't know what to believe." I told Tamara about my appointment with George Agonistes. "With any luck there'll be something inside the house to give us some answers."

"Better hope *she's* not inside, you know what I'm saying?"

"Worst-case scenario. Let's not go there."

"What about the kid?" Tamara asked. "You and Kerry gonna keep her at your place?"

"Until her mother turns up one way or another. She's got no place else to go."

"Yeah. You tell her about her folks?"

"Not yet."

"Gonna tell her?"

"Somebody's got to," I said. "I'd damn well prefer it to be her mother."

"Couldn't pay me enough for a job like that."

Enough on that subject. I said, "The Archie Todd case. What'd you turn up?"

"Plenty," she said. "Murdered or not, that old man sure got himself taken before he died. Screwed out of his life savings — every last penny."

"Inco and John Klinghurst."

"Phony investment scam, right. I called up Dunbar Asset Management yesterday. They didn't want to tell me anything, but I silver-tongued the dude who handled Archie Todd's account. Closed out in full in late September."

"So that's it."

"That's it. He wouldn't tell me how much Todd had or what he did with his holdings, but you just know he transferred everything straight to Inco of California."

"What about Klinghurst? Who is he?"

"CPA. Partner in a small outfit called Business Services, Inc. Offices on outer Geary. Another CPA with a get-rich-quick scheme, same as Emily's old man. And everybody thinks accountants are dull and boring."

"Does my mother-in-law know him?"

"Said she'd heard the name but couldn't place where. She'll get back to us if she remembers."

"Captain Archie's tax accountant, maybe."

"She said no. Man did his own taxes."

"Connected to the lawyer, Evan Patterson?"

"Not according to him. Told me he didn't know anything about Mr. Todd pulling out of Dunbar, never heard of Inco of California or John Klinghurst. I didn't come up with any facts that'd make him a liar."

"What's Klinghurst's past history?"

"No police record, city, state or federal. Some trouble with the IRS a few years ago, when he had his own agency — suspicion of collusion to defraud — but he was never prosecuted. Fast and loose type. Business Services, Inc., has that rep, too."

"His private life?"

"Divorced five years ago, no kids. Been at the Kirkham address about that long. Bought himself a brand-new Lexus last month. Not much doubt where he got the money for it."

"There has to be some tie to Captain Archie, Redwood Village."

"None I could find."

"The ex-wife?"

"Nothing there. She moved out of state after the divorce."

"Well, there's a connection somewhere," I said. "We don't have enough evidence to nail Klinghurst for fraud, or even to stir up an official investigation. Murder's a strong possibility, all right, if Captain Archie realized he'd been cheated and threatened to blow the whistle, but there's nothing to back it up or to involve Klinghurst. The missing link is how he and Todd got together in the first place."

"I'll keep working on it, blow off my afternoon classes if I have to. No problem."

"Up to you. Meanwhile I'll check out Klinghurst's neighbors."

"That mean you're coming back up here now?"

"I might as well. I'm not meeting Agonistes until five — that's seven hours, and there's not much I can do down here to fill up the time." Except run around talking to people who wouldn't want to see me and wouldn't be likely to tell me anything they might know — people like the three rumored past lovers of Sheila Hunter, and Smith again in person, and Doc Lukash and Anita Purcell and Richard Twining and any other member of the country club set who knew Mrs. Hunter. Frustrating waste of time, without either leverage or conclusive knowledge. And potentially counter-productive. If there were no leads in the Hunter house, then tomorrow I'd have to bite the bullet and start making the rounds. But not until then.

"Want me to try Mrs. Wade again?" Tamara asked.

"No. Prodding her will only get her back up."

"I like that old lady, you know? Reminds me of my granny. Tough old meat with a real sweet center."

I laughed. But Tamara was serious.

"We gonna nail this bastard Klinghurst for her, boss, one way or another. Slimeballs that prey on old people, take their money and what little time they got left, they're the worst breed of lowlife there is."

"Amen to that. You know something, Ms. Corbin?"

"What's that?"

"I like *you*. Tough young meat with a real sweet center."

18

San Francisco is essentially two cities when it comes to weather. East of Twin Peaks, the downtown area, is the sunny side, where warming air and wind currents scrub the skies clean on most dry days. West of Twin Peaks, the largely residential ocean side, is the fogbelt where you can spend days, even weeks shivering under a chill gray canopy and never once see the sun. San Franciscans get used to this phenomenon, which is not to say they like it much if they're westsiders. My flat is on the sunny side and Kerry's condo is atop Twin Peaks, right on the dividing line, but I was born out near Daly City and I know all too well what it's like being one of the "fog people."

The Inner Sunset is also on the gray side, close to Golden Gate Park and the upper reaches of the Haight-Ashbury. Old San Francisco, less dramatically changed than some parts of the city but still undergoing a slow metamorphosis. The rising Asian population in the Outer Sunset has spread inland from the ocean; many of the faces and small businesses on Irving Street, the neighborhood's commercial hub, are Chinese. Panhandlers and dope peddlers work the area now, and there is evidence of graffiti, vandalism, the subtler forms of urban decay. Still, it's a reasonably safe and comfortable area to live in as long as you don't mind the weather.

The fog was in, thick and dripping, when I pulled up in front of John Klinghurst's building a few minutes past eleven. The architecture here was mixed, everything from one of the brown-shingled cottages built in the aftermath of the 1906 earthquake to newish, five-and six-story apartment buildings. Klinghurst's was a narrow, two-story, stone-faced edifice that had probably been somebody's private home back in the twenties. There are a lot of places like that in the city, most of them cut up into two, three, or four flats, or several tiny apartments. This one housed four flats, two up and two down: there were four mailboxes in the cramped vestibule. Klinghurst lived upstairs, in 2-A.

I was looking at the other names, hunched

against the cold, when a woman came out of one of the ground-floor flats inside. She seemed to be in a hurry; she shoved through the entrance so quickly that I had to backpedal and go down a step to keep the door from whacking into me. She was on the short side, wiry, with iron-gray hair straggling out from under a shapeless hat, a straight-backed carriage, and an unlined, young-old face. She could have been any-where from sixty to eighty. She wore tennis shoes, Levi's, a flannel shirt, and a thin sweater — no coat or gloves, in spite of the fact it was that kind of day here.

I said, "Excuse me, ma'am. If you don't mind I'd like a few minutes of your time."

Bright blue eyes scowled at me. Snap, crackle, and pop eyes. "I do mind," she said in a voice to match. "If you're selling some-thing, you'd better get out of my way. I don't like solicitors."

"I'm not a solicitor. I have some questions about one of your neighbors."

"Which one?"

"John Klinghurst."

"That asshole. You a friend of his?"

"No, I'm not."

"What are you then?"

"A private investigator. I — "

"Hah!" she said, and I couldn't tell if she

meant anything by it or not. "I don't have time to stand around and chew the fat. I'm going to the market. You want to ask me questions, you'll have to walk along with me."

She didn't wait for an answer; she pushed past me — energetically, not rudely — and went down the steps and set off at a brisk pace. I had to hustle to catch up with her. She was short and she took short strides, but she covered a lot of ground in a hurry.

"Market's three blocks," she said. "Think you can keep up?"

"No problem." But I had to work a little just the same.

"Walking's good for you. Good for the heart, good for the lungs and leg muscles." She gave me a sidelong glance. "Good for trimming off fat, too. You ought to do more of it."

"Yes, ma'am."

"Don't call me ma'am. My name is Farber, Alice Farber."

"I'm pleased to meet you, Ms. Farber."

"No you're not, but at least you're polite. Not like that asshole you're investigating. Why are you anyway?"

"Investigating Klinghurst? Well — "

"Screwed somebody, probably, and I don't mean sex. He's the type. No scruples, no manners. He once called me a sorry old bitch to my face."

"What'd you call him back?"

"A prick with ears." She laughed. "He didn't like it."

"I'll bet he didn't."

"Well? You didn't answer my question."

"I think he screwed somebody, just as you said." She wasn't one to mince words; I saw no reason why I should. "Scammed a friend of my mother-in-law's out of his life savings."

"Hah! I knew he was that kind! Why hasn't he been arrested?"

"No proof yet."

"Better get plenty of it so some asshole lawyer doesn't get him off. Think you'll have it before the end of the month?"

"I hope so."

"Good. I'd like to be there when the cops come for him."

"Are you going somewhere at the end of the month?"

"No," she said, "he is. Moving out. I was happy to hear it, but this is better. Jail's where he'll be moving to now."

We'd reached the corner. An uncontrolled corner, with cars parked at the curb on the downhill side so you had an obstructed view of oncoming traffic. Alice Farber marched right out into the wet street with only a cursory glance to her left. It startled me and it must have scared hell out of the driver of a blue van, who jammed on his brakes and then blew his horn long and loud. It didn't faze her, though; she kept right on going without hesitation, up onto the sidewalk again with me at her heels like a balky dog.

"Kamikaze drivers," she said. "No discipline, no courtesy. Pedestrians always have the right of way in crosswalks."

There was nothing to say to that. I wouldn't have said it if there was. I asked, "Do you know where Klinghurst plans to move to?"

"Marin County."

"Where in Marin?"

"Don't ask me. Ask his real estate agents."

"You know who they are?"

"Thomas and Thomas, San Rafael. He got a big envelope from them last week." She threw me another sidelong glance. "Don't go thinking I poke around in other people's business. I don't. I came out one morning while the mailperson was there. She has packages, big envelopes, and she sees a tenant inside, she hands them over and the tenant puts them on a table in the lobby. You understand?"

"Sure. About this real estate outfit — "

"Thomas and Thomas. I happened to notice the name on the envelope, I remembered it because it was double. Husband and wife, two brothers, two sisters."

"Or partners who happen to have the same last name."

"Smart, aren't you?"

"Not as smart as I'd like to be. You wouldn't happen to know if Klinghurst is buying or renting?"

"Wouldn't I? I heard him telling Peterson, one of the other tenants, that he's buying property over there. Bought a new car, bought a house — all with that money you say he stole."

"Probably so."

"I hope he gets twenty years," she said. Then she said, "Who'd marry somebody like him? Another poop chute, must be."

"Klinghurst is getting married?"

"Isn't that what I said?"

"Do you know the woman's name?"

"How would I know? I told you, I don't poke around in other people's business."

"Did he ever bring her to his flat?"

"If he did, I never saw her. Or heard 'em going at it, either. His flat's right above mine and I probably would've."

We crossed another uncontrolled intersection, in the same headlong fashion as before, but uneventfully this time. Alice Farber, kamikaze pedestrian.

Pretty soon she said, "Flea market. What do you bet?"

"Flea market?"

"Where he met her. The poop chute he's marrying."

"Why do you say that?"

"Because that's what he does on weekends. Goes to flea markets all over the Bay Area, buys a lot of old junk and lugs it home. His flat's full of it. Take two moving vans to get all the crap out of there."

I wondered if Captain Archie had been a regular at Marin flea markets, if that was how he and Klinghurst had hooked up. I asked Ms. Farber, "Does Klinghurst have any interest in ferryboats?"

"In what?"

"Ferryboats. Ferryboat memorabilia."

"Are you serious? Or just yanking my shank?"

"Dead serious."

"How would I know? Ferryboats, for Chrissake."

I let it go. It wasn't worth the effort it would take to explain.

"There's the market." Another glance my way as she picked up speed and I worked to stay with her. "Puffing like a steam engine," she said in a pleased voice. "You're out of shape, mister."

I could have argued with her; I was not really puffing and I was in better shape than ninety percent of men my age. But that wasn't worth the effort, either. I just nodded and smiled and shrugged.

"Get more exercise," she said, "move those chubby buns of yours a mile or two every day, rain or shine. You'll look better, feel better, live longer."

"That's good advice."

"Damn right it is. You get that proof you need quick, you hear? Put that asshole in prison where he belongs." She swung away toward the market entrance. I followed her, and when she realized it she stopped and put those snap, crackle, and pop eyes on me again. "Where do you think you're going?"

"Inside."

"Too cold out here for you?"

"No. It's almost noon, and if they have a deli counter — "

"They have one, but you don't need deli food. Yogurt and an apple's what you should be eating for lunch."

"Yogurt and an apple. Right."

"And if you're thinking about waiting around and offering to carry my groceries home for me, don't. I wouldn't like it."

I hadn't been thinking of waiting around, but I didn't say so. I said, "Okay if I ask one more question?"

"As long as you make it quick."

"What do you do for a living, Ms. Farber? Or what did you do if you're retired?"

"That's two questions."

"Not really. Same question, asked two different ways."

"Smart," she said approvingly. "What do you think I did?"

"I don't have a clue."

"Go ahead, take a guess."

"Physical fitness instructor?"

"Wrong."

"Teacher?"

"Wrong again. Career officer, Women's Army Corps. Lieutenant Colonel when I took my retirement eight years ago." She squared her shoulders, gave me a sharp salute, executed a perfect about-face, and marched into the market.

The Golden Gate Bridge was packed with fog as thick as steel wool; it was not until I got to the bottom of Waldo Grade on the Marin side that the mist thinned out. In San Rafael it was clear and breezy, a nice, crisp autumn day. I stopped at a Shell station on Grand Avenue to check the phone directory.

Thomas & Thomas, Real Estate was on Second Street, which meant downtown and not far away.

It felt funny, being in San Rafael again and on my way to a downtown real estate firm. Brought too many painful memories up close to the surface. Bobbie Jean Addison worked in just such an agency, also not far away. At least, I assumed she still worked there; I'd had no contact with her in over a year, wanted none, and yet I could not help wondering what she was doing and how she was coping with memories far more painful and terrible than mine. It had taken me a while to put Eberhardt's suicide behind me, and we had been ex-partners and ex-friends for several years before he died. Bobbie Jean had lived with him, loved him, known things about him that I'd found out only after the fact, and watched him destroying himself slowly long before the final act and her part in it. She'd never be able to put up the kind of wall I had; hers would be the wailing kind, the nightmare kind you can neither tear down nor pass beyond. She was a strong woman, and she'd get through somehow, maybe even find snatches of peace and happiness, but she would never be the woman she'd once been, the happy-go-lucky Bobbie Jean I'd known.

Depressing thoughts. I squashed them down by concentrating on the little con I was going to run at Thomas & Thomas.

They were a small outfit, in a strip mall near where Second forks over and joins Fourth heading out toward San Anselmo. The usual plate-glass front window had the usual array of photographs of properties for sale, and a helpful listing in smaller letters below the agency name:

Michael J. Thomas
Claire M. Thomas

Inside I found one occupied desk and three empty ones. The lone occupant was a young woman wearing harlequin glasses, who was talking on the phone and tapping earnestly on a computer keyboard at the same time. She smiled at me and made a gesture to indicate she would be right with me; I smiled back and nodded and went to look at more photographs.

Three or four minutes of that, and the woman finally ended her conversation and turned her attention to me. "Yes, sir, how may I help you?"

"Are you Mrs. Thomas?"

"No, my name is Laura Vincent. Mr. and Mrs. Thomas are both out with clients. Is there something I can do?"

"Well, yes, I hope so. My name is Marlowe,

Phil Marlowe — I'm a friend of one of your agency's clients. John Klinghurst."

"Mr. Klinghurst. I don't . . . oh, yes, one of the buyers of the home in Los Ranchitos."

"That's right. Just recently."

"Yes, it's still in escrow."

"Well, he's pretty excited about it, been talking it up to everybody he knows. Raving is a better word. He really loves it."

Ms. Vincent's smile grew broader. "We're always pleased to hear that about one of our clients."

"He was so complimentary, in fact, that I thought I'd stop by and see if you had any other listings in that area. I live in the city, too, but I'm over here on business, so . . ."

"You're interested in buying a new home, then?"

"My wife and I, yes. We're tired of the rat race — city living grinds you down after a while."

"It certainly can. Have a seat, Mr. Marlowe, and let's see what we can do for you."

Tap, tap, tap on her computer keyboard. They didn't have any other Los Ranchitos listing, which made things a little easier for me. I asked what they had that was similar to the property Klinghurst had purchased, which prompted her to pull up his file to refamiliarize herself with the parcel. While she was doing that, I said casually, "How does it work when a man and his fiancée buy property together before they're married? I mean, do they put it in both their names — her maiden name, I mean — or just his or what?"

"Well, that depends . . ."

"How did John and Helen do it?"

I didn't have to prod her any more than that; she was curious enough herself to press the right button. Then she frowned and said, "Helen?"

"Helen Tolliver."

"It is a joint purchase," Ms. Vincent said, "but that isn't the name of the other party."

"You're kidding," I said. "You mean it's *not* Helen he's marrying? That's a shock, believe me. They've been going together off and on for years, and I just assumed . . . It's not Ann Burns, is it? I sure hope not."

"No. The name here is Jocelyn Dunn."

"Well, well," I said, "that's a real surprise," and I was no longer acting.

"Do you know her, Mr. Marlowe?"

"I've met her. Just once, but that was enough."

At Redwood Village, last Saturday afternoon.

Jocelyn Dunn, the big blonde nurse with the D-cup chest — a woman with easy access to both prescription medicine and Captain Archie Todd.

19

On my way to Larkspur I called Tamara to tell her what I'd discovered on the Todd case. She had some news for me on the Hunter case in return.

"Crazybone Cotter is still alive," she said, "still living in Billington, Illinois. But my guess is, his hunting days are over. As of Christmas Eve two years ago. Man had a stroke, left him mostly paralyzed."

"Brain damage?"

"No word on that. Pretty much bed-ridden, though. Wife number three's taking care of him. Ellen Coombs, a.k.a. Sheila Hunter, was number two. He divorced her a year after she split, grounds of desertion."

"Any publicity on the bond theft or her running off with Pete Stoddard?"

"Not a whisper. Whole thing was covered up."

"How about links between Cotter and organized crime?"

"Oh, yeah. He was brought up on money-laundering charges by the feds in '96, tried and acquitted for lack of evidence the following year."

"Strong mob ties?"

"Didn't come out that way. His lawyer didn't seem to be connected, either. Just a poor innocent victim of bad judgment, man claimed, and the jury believed him."

"Uh-huh."

"Not long after the trial he sold his manufacturing company outright to some Chicago outfit, maybe controlled by the wiseguys, maybe not. No way I could find out for sure." Wiseguys. Tamara tossed off slang terms like that as casually as a seasoned task-force vet. Working for me hadn't educated her that way; her father was a Redwood City police lieutenant. "Also couldn't turn up anything on whether Cotter's still connected or if the feds are still investigating him."

"My guess would be no on both counts," I said. "The trial publicity would've made him useless as a laundryman, and without strong ties they'd have cut him loose in a hurry. Doesn't matter in any case, as far as we're concerned."

"What about the Hunters?" she asked. "I mean, I got all of this stuff pretty much straight off the Net. They must've been keeping tabs on Cotter all along, right? Wouldn't make any sense for them not to."

"I figure they were, but what you and I read into the information and what they read into it are two different things. They may have relaxed some after Cotter's stroke — Jack Hunter, at least. That's probably why he let Twining talk him into taking out the life insurance policy. He was the smarter and more level-headed of the pair, the glue that held them together all those years. Without him she just couldn't handle the pressure, and her fear and paranoia took over."

"Suppose you don't find her, alive or dead? Suppose nobody does? What happens to the kid then?"

"I don't know," I said. "Tamara, I just don't know."

At Redwood Village I parked in the visitors' lot and walked over to the double-winged building that housed the rec center, dining hall, administration offices, and clinic. Before I went to tell Cybil the news about Jocelyn Dunn and John Klinghurst, I wanted to check with Dr. Lengel on a couple of things: whether Dunn had been on duty the night Archie Todd died, and whether a supply of the pink, 0.10 digitoxin pills was kept on hand at the clinic. The more information I had when I talked to Evan Patterson and then to the local authorities, the more likely it would lead to an immediate official investigation.

But I didn't get to talk to Lengel. Turned out this was one of his days off. And the physician on duty was out visiting a patient. The desk nurse was not Jocelyn Dunn, fortunately, though I learned Dunn was on the premises today. When I identified myself as a detective and the relative of a resident, the desk nurse consented to answer my question about the digitoxin. Affirmative. I didn't ask the other question; there was not much chance she would check a past duty roster without permission. Let police investigators follow through on that one.

From the clinic I walked through the landscaped grounds to Cybil's bungalow. The sun was out, but it was windy and cool; the only other people I saw were two elderly joggers in sweatsuits and a gardener making a lot of noise and fouling the air with a leaf blower. Leaf blowers and back-up beepers are two of my pet peeves. Gross noise polluters, both, the intrusive kind that grate on your nerves after a while. If it were up to me, the inventors of both would be locked up in enclosed spaces with the things going non-stop until they either went deaf or admitted their sins and vowed to invent quieter re-placements.

I walked faster, not that you can escape a racket like that on foot. And when I got to Cybil's, I saw that the front door of her unit stood partway open. It gave me pause. The day was too chilly for open doors, and I hap-pened to know that she had little tolerance for drafts or flies. I climbed the three steps, knocked and called out her name just as the leaf blower went mercifully silent.

Inside, somebody made a low, groaning sound.

I shouldered my way in, fast, squinting because the light in there was dim. The liv-ing room looked as though a small tornado had come swirling through. End table top-pled, coffee table kicked askew, lamp and books and sofa pillows and a scatter of other items over the carpet. The sofa had also been knocked sideways — and a pair of bent legs and foot were poked out be-hind it.

I sucked in a breath and ran over there. And then stopped and stood gawping a little with both confusion and relief, because the woman down there on the floor was not Cybil.

Nurse Jocelyn Dunn.

She lay sprawled on her back, one hand curling and uncurling spasmodically, her head twitching from side to side. There was a puffy bruise on her left temple, another on her cheekbone, and two or three cuts leaking blood in thin streams down into her gray-blond hair. Her eyelids were at half-mast, the eyes rolled up so that only the whites showed. She made another groaning sound; the curling and uncurling, the head twitching, went on unchecked. Conscious, barely, but not aware of me or anything else.

I veered away from her, to look into the kitchen. After that I checked the bedroom, bathroom, study, and peered out into the back patio. No sign of Cybil. In the living room again I took a quick second look at Nurse Dunn. The blood on her was fresh; she hadn't been there very long. Then I ran out onto the front porch, thinking to try next door —

And there was Cybil, just walking out of Captain Archie's place across the street.

She stopped when she spotted me and stood waiting as I ran over to her. Some sight she was, too. Hair disheveled, face flushed, eyes as bright as new pennies. In one hand she carried the bald-knobbed hickory walking stick that had belonged to her late husband. She didn't need it to get around; she'd kept it for sentimental reasons, and possibly for use as an emergency weapon. She was holding it weaponlike now, in the middle with the big knobbed head jutting forward.

"Cybil, are you all right?"

"Of course I'm all right. What are you doing here?"

"Never mind that now. What happened?"

"I saw you come out of my bungalow. Is that woman still unconscious?"

"More or less. You did some job on her — looks like she has a concussion. What'd you hit her with, that stick?"

"This? No. I brought it along for protection. I didn't want to call the police from my phone, in case she came to, so I took her master key and came over here to do it. They're on the way. I told them to bring an ambulance — "

"Will you please tell me what happened?"

"That fat cow tried to smother me, that's what happened. With one of my own sofa pillows."

"Why, for God's sake?"

"To shut me up, of course. *She's* the one who murdered Captain Archie. Her and her boyfriend, John Klinghurst."

"I know all that. I — "

"You know it? How did you find out?"

"By doing what you asked me to. Investigation. How did *you* find out?"

"I finally remembered where I'd heard the Klinghurst name," Cybil said. "Dunn was showing off a ring to Dr. Lengel a few months ago, while I was at the clinic. She said her fiancée gave it to her. Klinghurst is an unusual name and it stuck in the back of my mind. So when I saw her right after I remembered, I invited her in for a cup of coffee. I thought I'd do a little detective work myself. I guess I went too far and tipped my hand."

"I guess you did. Why didn't you call me instead of putting yourself at risk — "

"Don't scold me. I made a mistake, don't you think I know that?"

"You're lucky to be alive. How'd you manage to get away from her?"

"Samuel Leatherman. He saved my bacon."

I blinked at her. "Did you say — ?"

"That's just what I said. I wouldn't be here if it weren't for him."

"Cybil . . . are you sure you didn't get a whack on the head yourself?"

"Don't be silly. I'm perfectly fine."

"Then what're you talking about? You mean you used one of the tricks Leatherman uses in your stories?"

"No, that is not what I mean. I mean," she said slowly and distinctly, as if she were trying to get a point across to a halfwit, "that Samuel quite literally saved my life."

"And just how did he do that?"

"The same way he dealt with the murderer in *Dead Eye*, essentially. He and I smacked that top-heavy tramp upside the head and kept right on smacking her until she was out cold."

"Cybil . . ."

"My book, you ninny," she said with a mixture of exasperation and triumph. "*That's* what I picked up and hit the woman with while she was trying to smother me — my brag copy of *Dead Eye*."

I stayed with Cybil for a few minutes after the police left and the ambulance took a semicoherent Jocelyn Dunn off to the hospital. Not that Cybil needed me, once I'd added what I knew to her statement about the nurse, John Klinghurst, and Captain Archie. As a matter of fact, she barely knew I was there. She was surrounded by an eager crowd of other residents, regaling them with a salty account of Dunn's attack and her

Samuel Leatherman counteroffensive. She listened when I told her I was leaving to keep an appointment — it was after three by then — but only long enough to nod and then give me a peck on the cheek. She was holding court again as I walked away.

She'd said she would tell Kerry what had happened, but I figured it would be better if Kerry heard it from me first. I called her on the way out of Larkspur.

"I really shouldn't be surprised," she said when she got over the initial shock. "We both know that's the way Cybil is — headstrong, a fighter, and absolutely fearless."

"You forgot shameless."

"I didn't forget it, I just didn't say it. What do you bet she turns up on the evening news, and uses the opportunity to plug her book?"

"No bet." A local TV news van had been pulling into the lot as I was leaving it. "Guaranteed."

Tough old meat, all right, I was thinking fondly. As tough as it comes. And I wasn't too sure anymore about what Tamara had called the real sweet center.

20

I needn't have hurried getting down to Greenwood; George Agonistes turned up twenty-five minutes late for our appointment. I was in the fidgety, clock-watching stage of waiting when his unmarked white van finally pulled into the library lot. I got out to talk to him as he swung into an adjacent space.

"Sorry about that," he said. "I got hung up."

"I was beginning to think you weren't going to show."

"I never stand up paying customers. You bring me cash?"

"After you do the job."

"Sure. How far is it?"

"Not far. I'd ride with you, but you probably want to make a fast getaway before I do what I have to."

"See no evil," Agonistes said piously. "Lead on."

I led on. A woman was walking a standard poodle near the foot of the Hunters' driveway. She stopped to look as I made the turn, so I smiled and waved at her; she waved back. When I got up to the parking area, the white van grinding along on my tail, I glanced into the rearview mirror. The woman was still in sight, her attention on the poodle taking himself a squat by the side of the road. I considered it a positive sign that she found her dog crapping of greater interest than tandem visitors to the Hunter home.

Everything here was status quo; I'd swung by before going to the library to make sure. I joined Agonistes, who stood looking over the property with a jealous eye, his thin, gnarly body bent against the wind, his wild thatch of Don King-style hair blowing in different directions.

"How the other half lives," he said. "Must be nice."

"Not necessarily."

He opened up the back of the van to unload his tool kit. The interior was jammed with every conceivable variety of sophisticated electronics equipment, both manufactured and self-made. Starlight nightscopes, motion detectors hooked up to infrared still and video cameras, FM wireless and infinity transmitters, recording and debugging devices, laser shotguns and surveillance spike mikes — you name it and he owned it. In his own minor way, he was something of a techno genius.

We went to the front door and he spent about ten seconds studying the alarm pad. "Uh-huh," he said, and went to peer at the nearby windows, and came back and said, "No sweat. Fifteen minutes, tops."

"My hero. Just don't set the damn thing off."

He looked offended. "You won't hear it if I do. It's the silent type."

"But you'd know if you did set it off?"

"Cut it out. I don't make that kind of mistake." He opened his tool kit. "You might want to watch what I do. In case you run up against this kind of situation again."

"No, thanks. I wouldn't know what I was seeing. I need an instruction manual to change a light bulb."

I went over to where I had an oblique view of the street below. The woman and her poodle were gone; only his calling card remained. A few cars rumbled by, none of them official-looking, and there was no other pedestrian traffic.

After twelve minutes by my watch, Agonistes called my name. He was closing up his tool kit when I reached him. The alarm pad looked exactly as it had before, the plate tight-screwed to the wall; the only difference was that now the red light was off.

"That'll be two hundred and fifty bucks," he said.

"I don't suppose you know an easy way to get past a dead-bolt lock."

"Not my area of expertise. Whatever you do to get inside, you won't have to worry about alerting the M.A.S. command center. Pay me and I'm out of here."

I paid him. "I wish I had your hourly rate."

"Sure you do. What you wouldn't want are my expenses."

"I'll be in touch, George."

"Uh-huh. Next time you've got a job for me, try to make it at least semilegal."

"Why should I be different than any of your other clients?"

He waved and went away. I was glad to see him go. I liked Agonistes and most times I didn't mind the mandatory raillery our relationship seemed to require, but I had little patience for it tonight. I was edgy about getting into the house, edgy about what I might find in there.

Dusk was approaching now and that meant I'd have to put lights on inside, something else that made me uneasy. I looped around to the rear, checking windows along the way; all of them were tightly latched. There was a set of steps leading up to a back deck. I climbed up there and tried the sliding-glass doors I found. They wouldn't budge. Double-locked, likely — regular latch and a security bolt at the bottom or top.

No more time to waste. And only one real option anyway. I descended the steps and went around on the side away from Whiskey Flat Road. The branches of the heritage oak and a row of cypress shrubs separating the property from its nearest neighbor gave me as much privacy as I'd need. I picked one of the windows toward the back, the smallish kind that usually means bathroom; a shade was drawn over it so I couldn't see inside. I waited until the wind gusted and made some noise in the trees and then drove my elbow in a short, hard thrust against the lower pane. The glass shattering seemed loud, but it wasn't loud enough to carry. I cleared out shards with my elbow, widening the hole, then reached through and found the latch and raised both the sash and the shade.

Right: bathroom. I wiggled my way through, being careful of the broken glass. A

child's robe hung from the back of the closed door; a jar of bubble bath and a rubber Donald Duck bath toy sat on the edge of the tub. Emily's bathroom. It made me feel like even more of an intruder, as if I were violating a place I had no right to be. Emily would have understood, but I wished just the same that I'd picked a different window.

I passed through her neat bedroom — stuffed animals dominated it, all shapes and sizes — and into a central hallway. I stood there for a little time, keening the air like a dog, getting the feel of the house. It didn't feel right, but that could have been my keyed-up state, the fact that I was in the process of an illegal trespass for the third time in four days, even a reaction to the faint musty smell that develops in places closed up for more than a couple of days.

First action, then, was a quick preliminary search, opening doors and switching on lights and shutting them off again. Three bedrooms, three full baths, den, TV room, formal living room, family room, dining room, kitchen, utility room with washer and dryer. Computers, TV sets, VCR's, stereo system with six-foot speakers, wet bar loaded with expensive Scotch, bourbon, and gin, fancy household gadgets, child's toys and adult toys, fashionable clothing, a smattering of antiques — everything that illicit money could buy to take the place of faith, stability, unity, peace of mind. Expendable leftovers now. Throwaways. Emily's hollow, inconsequential legacy.

Otherwise, the house was empty.

Orderly, clean, and empty — no signs of disturbance anywhere.

There should have been a small relief in that. Ever since yesterday I'd had a nibbling suspicion that I might find Sheila Hunter dead in here. Not the case, yet I couldn't shake the not-right feeling. It was like a colorless toxic gas that you couldn't quite smell or taste. Something had happened here. A violent act, possibly, despite the apparent lack of supportive evidence. Violence leaves that kind of residue, a psychic stain on the atmosphere. A touch of evil.

I prowled through the rooms again, stopping in the den and then the master bedroom to search closets and drawers and paper files. Nothing to tell me where Sheila Hunter might have gone, or who the third party involved in her disappearance might be. And all the while my sensitivity to the residue of evil grew until I was drawn so tight inside I could hear myself fast-ticking like an overwound clock.

Back to the front of the house. The

residue seemed concentrated in that part; the hairs on my neck prickled as I walked through the living room. Not in there, though. Nor in the family or dining room.

Kitchen.

I flipped on the overhead track lights and stood in the archway, looking in. Big, open kitchen, usual appliances, wood-block center island with an electric stove top and tiled counter space alongside. Clean and tidy, like the rest of the house. Sheila Hunter was a far better housekeeper than her sister.

Nothing wrong, nothing out of place — or was there? The longer you look at a particular area, the more details your eyes pick out. The first one that caught my awareness was a toaster on the countertop next to the sink. Two pieces of bread in it, popped up, dark brown. Nearby sat a plate, empty except for a fork. Above a tiered pair of wall ovens was a built-in microwave with its door partway open. A paring knife lay in one half of a double stainless-steel sink; a copper saucepan was in the other half. I saw those last two things when I moved a few paces toward the center island.

I kept on going to the toaster, felt one of the bread slices. Hard, brittle — been there a while. I bent to peer first at the paring knife; the blade was clean. The saucepan had been used to cook something with oil or grease in it. Even though it had been rinsed out, a faint smeary ring showed inside.

Sidestepping, I poked the microwave door all the way open. Within was a tray full of a congealed substance that on closer inspection turned out to be macaroni and cheese. Heated but never taken out. Also there for some time.

Under the sink was a garbage bag; I dragged it out and stirred among the contents with two fingers. Couple of wads of paper towel, the carton the macaroni and cheese had come in, an empty package that had contained Ballpark Franks, and a shriveled, cooked or partially cooked hot dog. I lifted the hot dog out and examined it, sniffed it. Nothing wrong with it that I could tell. Heated and then tossed in the garbage.

Little things. By themselves they didn't mean much, but when you added them all together . . .

I put the bag back where I'd found it, closed the cabinet doors. I was still humped over as I turned away from the sink, and the angle of my vision was just right for me to notice a faint smear on the blond-wood base of the island. It might have been grease or a food spatter, but it wasn't. I knew what it was even before I flaked a little of it off on my fingernail.

Blood. Dried blood.

The smear was down close to the floor, near one of the corners. Sharp corners, this one nicked and gouged in a couple of places as if something hard had banged into it. Up close the marks looked relatively fresh. I checked for more blood residue, didn't find any. The rest of the wood was clean, smelling of lemon scent, and the patterned linoleum floor underneath was also clean, as from a recent mopping. I got down on all fours and crawled around the island. The floor along the other three sides was not quite as spotless.

Away from me, against the baseboard under the bottom oven, something glittered.

I saw it as I started to get up. Whatever it was, it was tiny and yet it shone brightly in the track floodlights. I crawled over there and picked it up and laid it on my palm for a better look.

Thin piece of filigreed gold about an eighth of an inch long, bent on one end, jaggedly sheared on the other. Broken link from a bracelet or necklace, maybe. It hadn't been down there long: no grit or dust to dull the polished surface.

Slowly I got to my feet. All sorts of things

had begun to run around inside my head — facts, impressions, scraps of conversation dislodged from memory, irrelevancies that became relevant by short hop or quantum leap. My mind works that way sometimes, when it gets stuffed full enough — a kind of skip-around stream of consciousness that somehow sorts itself out into cohesiveness and clarity.

Dried blood and a broken gold link. Sharp corner, nicked and gouged, and a partly cleaned floor. Uneaten toast, uneaten macaroni and cheese. Half-clean pot in the sink, half-cooked frankfurter thrown away. Ballpark Franks — they plump when you cook 'em. DiGrazia's Old-Fashioned Italian Sausages — new world elegance, old world taste. Roseanna, she says I got sausage on the brain. I sure wish she'd let me bother her a time or two. That's all you ever think about, she says, your sausage. I can tell you this — she wouldn't play the one time I tested the waters. Cogliona *like that, hates you one minute, you talk to her right and the next minute maybe she changes her mind. Persistence is my middle name. Bada boom, bada bing, maybe she ends up sampling my sausage after all. Bombay Gin and Speyburn Scotch. Drowning herself in gin, as usual. I am a connoisseur of martinis, Charles, did you know that? I've got some really good twelve-year-old*

Scotch. She made his life miserable . . . cold-hearted bitch, someday I'll tell her what I think of her. Out somewhere that required looking her best. Drunks are unpredictable, can't tell what they might do. Bada bing, bada boom . . .

Little things, lots of them, and what they amounted to was something big and ugly. A chain reaction scenario of sudden violence, sudden death.

There was anger in me now, cold and focused. If my scenario was the right one, and I was reasonably sure it was, I had more work to do tonight. Hard work. Dirty work.

I went out of there to get it done.

21

Most businesses in the village were closed for the day; it was almost seven o'clock. The first open place I stopped at, a liquor store, had a public phone outside, but the directory was missing. I went inside long enough to ask the clerk a couple of questions about Speyburn single highland malt Scotch. Then I drove on a ways until I came to a Shell station.

Two phone booths there, one with a tattered book. I flipped through the survivor's white pages. There was a listing — an address on Ridgecrest Road. I had a map in the car that would tell me how to find it.

"He's not here," the woman said.

Her name was Lillian. She'd volunteered that information right after she opened the door, making it plain that she preferred her given name to her married one. Even in the pale porch light I could tell she had once been a beauty, the dark-haired, smoky type. She was still attractive at around forty, but there was a letting-go laxness to her facial muscles, a listlessness in her voice and movements, lines bracketing her mouth that had been deep-etched by the acid of bitterness. Behind her, inside the house, I could hear voices and laughter, some young and live, the rest canned — teenagers watching a TV sitcom.

"When do you expect him?" I asked.

"I don't. He'll be late, as usual."

"Do you know where he is? It's important I talk to him."

"Can't it wait until tomorrow?"

"No. It's urgent. Really."

Pause. "He said he had a business meeting."

"Did he say where or with whom?"

"No."

"So you haven't any idea where I can find him?"

Another pause, longer this time. Studying me. I was making an effort to keep my feelings from showing, but some of the anger must have leaked through. A good thing, as it turned out.

At length she said, "What do you want to talk to him about?"

"A personal matter."

"I see. An urgent personal matter."

"Very urgent."

Her faint smile had no humor in it; in the diffused light the lines of bitterness looked deep and blood-dark, like slash marks. She thought she knew what kind of urgent matter, that was plain. And it didn't seem to bother her. If anything, she was pleased. Long-suffering and fed up, and I'd caught her in just the right frame of mind.

"Well, then," she said, "I may have an idea where he is. I probably shouldn't tell you this, but he has a cabin up in the mountains off Skyline. It used to belong to his brother before Dennis moved to Texas. He goes up there sometimes."

"On business?"

The faint smile again, so fleeting this time it was like a shadow across her mouth. "When he wants to get away from me and the kids. His private little retreat."

"Can you give me directions?"

"It's about fifteen miles from here."

"I don't mind driving fifteen miles."

"You might have trouble finding it."

"I don't mind that, either."

She told me how to get there, in some detail. I said then, "A few more questions before I go. What kind of Scotch does your husband drink?"

"Now why would you want to know that?"

"Speyburn? The expensive twelve-year-old kind?"

"That's right. Nothing but the best for him."

"Is he in the habit of keeping a bottle in his car?"

"I wouldn't be surprised." Her laugh was as cold as the night. "He wouldn't want to be caught without it in an emergency. Such as a sudden business meeting. So you'd better be prepared, not that you aren't already."

"Prepared?"

"If he is at the cabin," she said, "he won't be alone."

Lillian's directions were explicit enough, but as she'd predicted I had a little trouble pinpointing the exact location of the cabin. It was northwest of Greenwood, on winding Tenitas Creek Road just off Skyline; the area was heavily forested, the property screened from the road by pine and spruce, the night dark, windy. Shifting splinters of light winked through the trees, but it wasn't until my second pass that I spotted the half-hidden driveway leading in that way. The drive made a dogleg to the left partway along so I couldn't tell whether the illumination came from a window or some kind of outside nightlight.

I drove past again and on down the road a few hundred yards, to where I'd U-turned the first time. Mine was still the only car in sight. I made another quick swing around, came back uphill in low gear. A short distance below the driveway, on my side of the road, my headlights picked up a narrow, rough-earth turnout. I cut the lights and eased in there, making certain I was all the way off the pavement before I shut off the engine.

I felt around under the dash, unsnapped the .38 Colt Bodyguard from its clips, and slid the gun into my pocket. Heavy darkness broken only by those distant shards of light enveloped me as I got out; the road was still deserted. Cold, pummeling wind, directionless night sounds, the strong resinous scent of evergreens and the more pungent flavor of woodsmoke. I pulled my coat collar up, ran across the road to the driveway.

It was of packed earth, rutted and overlain with a carpeting of pine needles. There was enough starshine overhead to outline the ruts and uneven ground between them; the tree shadow along both sides was as thick as black paste. I walked in as fast as I dared, head down and body bent so I could watch my footing. Dry needles and twigs crackled under my weight, but the wind made more than enough noise to drown out small sounds. The woodsmoke smell was stronger in there.

Off to my left the light grew less fragmented, and when the track began to curve, the trees thinned out and I could see part of a clearing, then the black bulk of the cabin. The light came from inside, making a warm yellow rectangle of a front window. In the outspill, there was the gleam of metal and glass — two cars parked before a narrow, railed porch, one medium-size and dark colored, the other low-slung and light colored.

Richard Twining was here, all right. And he wasn't by himself.

I changed course slightly, taking an angle that brought me to the cabin on the side away from the lighted window. Music played inside, not loud, just discernible above the skirl of the wind. I passed slowly alongside the sports car, ducked under the log rail at the far end and lifted up on the porch.

Boards creaked, but barely loud enough for me to hear. I took another step, and there was a wind gust that hammered a shutter or loose shingle somewhere, created a series of mutters and rattles and shushes in the trees. By the time it lulled again I was past the front door and up against the wall next to the lighted window.

Inside, a woman laughed suddenly, a shrill giggle that ended in a kind of squeal. Then the squeal became something else, a long, drawn-out sighing moan. I knew that sound, all right; there is no other like it and its cause is as old as time. I eased my head and body around, not being too cautious about it because there was no longer any need, and peered in through the glass.

They were on the floor in front of a stone fireplace, on a scatter of oversize throw pillows. Light from a log fire and a squatty end-table lamp shone on outflung arms and legs and bare, sweat-shiny flesh. The woman was on top, turned in profile to me — young, carrot-topped, plump, and enthusiastic; I had never seen her before. Twining's face was clearly visible, teeth bared, eyes open and lust-popped, a satyr's mask that turned my stomach. Under other circumstances I would have looked away immediately; I've never much cared for sex as a spectator sport. But it was not what they were doing that kept me standing there a few seconds longer. It was what I saw when he arched his body, twisted and lifted his head off the pillow: three parallel lines a couple of inches long, an angry red in the firelight and lampshine, on the left side of his neck down to the collarbone.

No doubt of it now, none at all. The anger in me boiled up, to the point where I did not give a damn about being reckless. I side-stepped to the door, felt for the knob, turned it. Not locked. Good. Less wear and tear on me.

I went in, making as much noise as I could, and slammed the door behind me.

22

There was nothing comical in the way they broke apart, surged up off the floor in a wild untangling of arms and legs and bumping of bodies. Or in the way the woman grabbed up one of the pillows to cover herself, making little frightened squeaking noises. Or in the way Twining gawked at me in those first few seconds, with slack-jawed incredulity and the clownlike foolishness of a middle-aged, paunchy stud caught in flagrante delicto. The whole scene was pathetic and shameful and disgusting. And I was loaded with too much dark and bitter rage.

He said, "You . . . what . . . Jesus Christ, how did you . . ." Confused and meaningless sputterings. He took a half-step toward me. "Son of a bitch . . ."

"Stay where you are." I had my hand in my coat pocket, holding on to the gun, but I did not want to show it unless I was forced to; the plump carrot-top had nothing to do with this and she was scared enough as it was. I moved the pocket a little, with just enough menace to show Twining I was armed and meant business. But it was all right. Very few naked men are willing to start trouble with another who is fully dressed, and he wasn't one of the few. Lover, big lover, not a fighter.

"Rich?" the woman said in querulous tones. "For God's sake, Rich?"

He paid no attention to her. "What the hell's the idea?" he said to me. Confusion giving way to blustery anger. And with the return of control came the realization that he was standing there nude in front of me. His gaze wavered and slid away, around behind him. His pants were draped across the back of a wicker sofa; he moved over there, trying not to be too eager about it, and managed to put them on without hopping around too much. That made him feel better. He came back to where he'd been before and glared at me and said, "What the fuck's the idea? Who do you think you are, busting in here like this?"

Ignoring him, I said to the woman, "Go into the bedroom and put your clothes on. Then get in your car and drive away. Your boyfriend and I have some business to take care of."

She looked at Twining, clutching the pillow against her body with both arms. "Rich?"

"Go on, get dressed," he said without looking at her. "I'll handle this."

"Are you sure — ?"

"Go on, go on!"

She went, scooping up clothing with one hand and then running. I didn't pay any attention to where she went; I had eyes only for Twining.

He said, "I don't have any goddamn business with you."

"Sheila Hunter."

". . . What?"

"You heard me. Sheila Hunter."

"I don't know what you're talking about." Bluff and bluster, but he couldn't keep the fear from showing in his eyes.

"How'd you get those scratches on your neck, Twining?"

His hand came halfway up, twitched, and went paralytically still. The fear was on his face now, in little beads of sweat. "I don't have to answer that. This is my house — you're trespassing on private property. I can have you arrested."

"Go ahead. Call the law."

"I will if you don't get out of here — "

"I'm not going anywhere. You're the one going somewhere."

"Bullshit." Then, "Where am I going?"

"You know where."

The carrot-top came back into the room like somebody walking on hot embers. Wearing a green coat, her hair still tangled, her eyes still showing fright — but not as much fright as Twining's.

"Should I leave?" she asked him. "Like he said?"

He licked his lips, ran the back of one hand across his forehead. "Go ahead, Tanya. I'll call you."

"Should I . . . I mean, do you want me to go straight home?"

I said, "She wants to know if she should call the law, tell them about me. She thinks you're in trouble."

"Rich? *Are* you in trouble?"

"No."

"Yes," I said. "But you don't want her to call anybody, do you? You just want her to go on home."

"*Is* that what you want, honey?"

"Yeah. Christ, just get out of here."

"You'll be okay? He won't do anything to — "

"Shut up! You stupid bitch, I can't think

with you yapping at me. Shut up and move your fat ass out of here."

He couldn't have hurt her more, or got her out of there more quickly, if he'd kicked her broad bottom. She went flying through the door, yelling "Fuck you!" over her shoulder, and banged it after her with enough force to dislodge a plaque from the knotty pine wall next to it.

Twining wheeled away and went to the fireplace. The fire was banking; he picked up a poker and bent and began to stir the charred wood around. As soon as he did that I took the .38 out of my pocket and held it down against my leg. Outside, a car engine came to life, revved up high. Headlights flashed on, glared through the window, then made a sweeping pattern across the far wall as the carrot-top backed her car around.

When she roared away I said to Twining, "Put the poker down and come back over — "

I didn't get the rest of it out because the damn fool was moving by then, swinging around and making a wild-eyed rush my way with the poker lifted high. I raised the gun, but he was too far gone to see it or to stop his charge if he did. But he hadn't surprised me any; I had plenty of time to set myself and then dodge sideways just as he started his downward swipe. The poker slashed air, nowhere close to me. The force of his lunge bent him over and his foot came slanting down on one of the throw rugs. It slid, he slid, and I stepped in and kicked his leg out from under him.

He went down yelling, but he didn't lose the poker. I backed off and shouted at him, "Don't get up, Twining!" Useless words; he was already flopping around, trying to set his legs under him. Only one thing I could do then, and I didn't waste any time doing it: I threw the gun up and squeezed off a round.

Not at him, at the far wall — a warning shot. The racket the .38 made was like a small explosion in there. To my relief it had the desired effect on Twining: It turned him stone-still on his knees, the tip of the poker still touching the floor.

"Let go of it," I said. "The poker. Let go. Don't make me put the next bullet in you."

He stared up at me out of those bulging eyes. I waggled the revolver at him. The wildness went out of his face; he jerked his hand free of the poker handle as if it had suddenly become red hot. "Jesus!" he said, and it was as close to a prayer as somebody like him would ever get.

"On your feet. Go sit on the sofa."

"You . . . oh . . . God, you could've killed me."

"That's right, I could have. But I like the alternatives better. Do what I told you."

He tried to get up, couldn't make it the first time. I watched him gather himself, struggle to his feet, stagger toward the wicker sofa. The last couple of steps were a lunge, as if his legs were giving out on him. He sat there with his teeth gritted, the sweat on his face shining in the dying firelight, looking at me and then not looking at me in little flicks of his head and eyes.

After a time he said, "I shouldn't've done that. Come at you like that. But the way you busted in here . . . and now that gun . . . What's the idea? What do you want?"

"You know why I'm here."

"I don't know. You said . . . alternatives. What alternatives?"

"Not the kind you're looking for. Prison. Maybe even lethal injection."

One side of his face spasmed, the rippling kind that pulled it out of shape. He pawed viciously at his cheek. "You're crazy! I haven't done anything."

"Just killed two women, that's all."

"I never killed anybody!" It was a shriek as shrill as the carrot-topped Tanya's parting shot, and with just as much anguish.

"Sheila Hunter and Dale Cooney."

"No. No!"

"I can prove it, Twining."

"No. How can you . . . no."

"Yes. The scratches on your neck, for one thing. Made by a woman's fingernails."

"My wife. Or Tanya . . ."

"Sheila Hunter. She clawed you, and when she did she broke the gold chain you wore around your neck. Same gold chain you had on the day I talked to you in your office. You missed one of the links when you cleaned up her kitchen. I found it. Found some other things you missed, too. Like a smear of her blood on the center island."

His throat worked as if he were going to be sick. He clamped his jaws to keep his gorge down, wiped his mouth, pawed at his face again. His eyes were as big and streaky-white as cocktail onions.

"Here's the way I think it happened," I said. "You went to her house on Saturday around noon, one o'clock. Pretense of business, but she was the real reason. Big stud like you, knowing she played around with Trevor Smith and any number of other guys but never with you — it must've been like a needle jabbing that cocksman's ego of yours. So you decided to give it one more try. Only she was strung out, scared, never mind why, and the pass you made set her off. I figure she called you names, maybe slapped you, maybe scratched you then, and that set *you* off. You lost control, threw her down, raped her right there on the kitchen floor — "

"No!" He had both hands up in front of him, palms out, as if he were trying to ward off my accusations. "I never raped her! I never raped any woman!"

"Then how did she die?"

He shook his head, hard.

"How did Sheila Hunter die, Twining?"

". . . Accident." The word came out convulsively, like a piece of something that had been choking him and that he'd hacked loose. It left him panting a little, so that his next words were broken and wheezy. "An accident, I swear to God . . . an accident."

"She just slipped and fell, I suppose. All by herself."

"It wasn't my fault."

"No? Tell me how it happened."

"I . . . all right. All right." Deep, shaky breath. "I talked my way into the house, made a pass at her . . . nothing heavy, I just nuzzled her a little. And she . . . I don't know, she just went crazy. Screamed at me, slapped my face. I shoved her away, but she came right back with those goddamn claws out, marked me, broke the chain. . . . But I didn't hit her, not even then. I shoved her away again, that's all, I swear it. It wasn't my fault. She was cooking something, hot dog in a pot, and she grabbed the pot and swung it at me. I couldn't get out of the way in time, fucking pot slammed my elbow and threw hot water all over me. Would've scalded me if it'd been boiling, but she hurt me enough as it was — "

"Hold it. Where'd you say she hit you with the pot?"

"My elbow. Right on the crazybone. Man, you must know how much that hurts, you get hit on the crazybone like that."

Sweet Jesus!

"I went a little crazy myself," he said. "Anybody would, getting marked and then hit like that. I smacked her. Sure, I smacked her . . . it was self-defense. You can see that, can't you? I smacked her good, right in the face, I was only trying to protect myself, and she went over backward and her head . . . ah, man, I can still hear the sound her head made when it hit that wood corner . . ." Twining's face screwed up for a few seconds, as if he might cry. If he had, the tears would not have been for Sheila Hunter; they would have been for Richard Twining. He dry-washed his face again, looked up at me pleadingly. "Dead. Caved in the back of her skull. There wasn't anything I could do for her. Eyes all rolled up into the back of her head, no pulse, blood in her hair . . . dead, just like that."

I didn't say anything. In my mouth was a taste like ashes and bile.

"An accident, a freak accident," Twining said. "But who'd believe it? She'd marked me, it happened in her house . . . I was scared. Scared and not thinking straight. At first I just wanted to get out of there, run like hell, but I couldn't do that with my gold chain all over the floor, my fingerprints Christ knew where . . . and suppose somebody'd seen me drive in? And I'd talked to Mack Judson about her, his office is next to mine and she'd called him about putting her house up for sale. That's why I went out to see her, I figured it was my last chance . . ." Headshake. "I *couldn't* just leave her there. I had to do something."

"So you cleaned up the kitchen and took her body away."

"What else could I do? It was the only thing I could think to do. I wrapped her up in some sheets and put her in the trunk of my car. I had her purse, her keys . . . I locked up the house, turned on the alarm system. Her car was in the garage but there wasn't anything I could do about that, I had to leave it where it was . . ."

"The body, Twining. What'd you do with it?"

Another headshake. He didn't want to talk about that.

"Buried her somewhere, is that what you did?"

No answer.

"Took her up here and buried her," I said. "Right here on this isolated property of yours."

A guess, but the right one. He twitched a little, looked away, looked back at me. "I didn't want to risk going anywhere else," in a hoarse whisper. "Back in the trees — "

"Don't tell me. Save it for the police."

"Police." The word produced a shudder. He sat there for a few seconds, abruptly tried to get up and then sank back down as if he had no strength. "Listen," he said, "I've got money, about thirty thousand in liquid assets and I can raise another hundred or so, more if I sell my house. It's yours, every penny, if you — "

"You can't buy my silence, Twining. You couldn't buy it for ten million dollars. Two women are dead and a little girl is an orphan because of you, and you're not going to pay for that with money."

"Two women? No," he said, "you're

wrong. Sheila Hunter, yeah, it was self-defense, I panicked, but nobody else . . ."

"Dale Cooney. Her you killed in cold blood."

"No! You can't pin that on me. She was a lush, she drove home drunk and passed out in her garage with the engine running . . . another accident, that's what everybody's saying . . ."

"Murder. Your murder."

"For Chrissake, why would I kill Dale Cooney?"

"I think she showed up at the Hunter house after Sheila Hunter died, while you were still there. Fortified with booze, mourning her lover, and looking to tell his widow what she thought of her. I think she saw you and your car, the scratches on your neck, maybe even you putting the body in the trunk."

"No."

"I think you used that glib, bullshit charm of yours to convince her nothing was wrong, get her to leave. But you were still in a panic, afraid she'd change her mind and contact the police. So you followed her home. Either she told you her husband was away for the weekend or you knew it some other way. Nobody else on the premises made it easy to hit her with something, arrange things to look like she'd passed out with the engine running. But you screwed up with the Scotch. She was a gin drinker, martinis. If you'd remembered that, you could've used her house key and gotten a bottle of her Bombay gin, but you wanted out of there and it was quicker to use the Speyburn — your brand of single malt, a bottle from your car. Might have one of your fingerprints on it, even if you did try to wipe it clean. Premeditated, first-degree murder."

"I didn't do any of that! I never saw Dale Cooney that day! I tell you I didn't kill her, I didn't have anything to do with it!"

Lies. I knew it and he knew I knew it, but he was not going to budge. I could almost see the wheels turning inside his head, the protective shell he was trying desperately to hold tight around himself. He'd admitted what happened with Sheila Hunter, but in his mind it was an accident, self-defense, not his fault, and nobody would ever convince him otherwise. He'd moved and buried her body, he was probably going to prison, but maybe a judge and jury would be inclined to leniency; he was a pillar of the community, he'd made a mistake and he was sorry and willing to pay for it, he'd throw himself on the mercy of the court.

But Dale Cooney's death was just what I'd

said it was — cold-blooded murder. Admit that, and he'd go to prison for the rest of his life, possibly even wind up on death row. Admit the truth, and it made him into something he couldn't face up to in either the public eye or his own eyes — it made him a kind of monster. So he'd deny it and he'd keep on denying it, the way the famous football player turned actor had denied guilt all through his trial and ever since. Nobody'd ever shake the truth out of Richard Twining, no matter what.

But *he* knew what he'd done. He'd have to live with the knowledge for the rest of his life, and even if the law couldn't find enough evidence to convict him of Dale Cooney's murder, he wouldn't escape punishment for it. He'd be punished plenty, sorry bastard that he was, in the cold, sleepless dark of the nights to come.

I'd had enough of him; I'd had too much of too many people like him who refused to accept responsibility for their actions. I said, "All right. Put on the rest of your clothes. It's time for the police."

"Listen," he said, "please, isn't there any way — ?"

"Not with me. Get dressed. Now."

He got slowly to his feet, reached out an unsteady hand for his shirt. Not looking at me, he said, "Sheila Hunter . . . honest to God, it was an accident. You tell the police that."

"Tell them yourself what you did or didn't do."

"I never saw Dale Cooney that day, I hadn't seen her in weeks, I didn't have anything to do with her dying. They have to believe me. They have to!"

I quit listening to him. Quit thinking about him. What I thought about, standing there waiting for him to finish dressing was Emily and what I would have to say to her pretty soon, the terrible things I would have to say to that little girl.

23

It was one of the hardest things I've ever had to do.

Kerry was there for moral support, but that did not make it any easier. I still had to say the words, and to look into those sad, lost eyes as I said them. Omitting the more sordid details didn't help, either. Nor did using softened phrasing and clichés and half-truths like "Your mom and dad did a bad thing once but they weren't bad people" and "What happened to your mom wasn't her fault; the man who killed her is sick, as sick as the one who hurt her before you were born." Kerry tried, too, in the same vein. "She loved you, she'd never have abandoned you" and "Your parents didn't tell you the truth because they wanted to protect you." Awkward, bitter, empty, comfortless words, every one.

Emily sat there and listened to them with

no outward emotion, without even flinching much — and maybe without really believing the clichés and half-truths. Her only reaction, when I broke the news about her mother, was to squeeze her eyes shut and say, "I knew she was dead." She spoke little after that. And when it was over I was the one who sat tense and sweating; her body was slack, her face and eyes clear and dry. She had already done most of her weeping, I thought, and if there were any more tears she would shed them quietly and alone. Her outward appearance was a child's protective armor. Inside, she had to be a mass of bruises — stoned and hurting from all those awkward, bitter, empty, comfortless words.

It was just as well neither Kerry nor I could think of anything more to say; silence was a few seconds of mercy. Emily was the one who finally ended it.

"Where will I go now?" she asked in a small voice.

"Nowhere, honey," Kerry said. "You'll stay right here with us."

"I mean later. Will I have to live with Aunt Karen?"

"No way," I said. "Don't worry about that."

"Not even if she comes back to her house?"

"No matter where she ends up."

"What about Uncle Mike?"

"I promise you that won't happen, either."

"Then where will I live? There isn't anyone else."

Kerry and I exchanged glances. She said, "What will probably happen is that you'll be made a ward of the court. Do you know what that means?"

"No."

"It means a judge will make the decision because you're not old enough yet. He'll work with a child welfare agency to find a foster family for you to live with."

"Strangers," Emily said.

"Yes, but a good family, with other kids your age — "

"I don't think I'll like that."

"Why not? Once you get to know them — "

"I don't make friends very well. I don't feel comfortable with people I don't know."

Amen, I thought.

Kerry said, "You feel comfortable with us, don't you?"

"You're different — you're older. I mean kids my age. Mom and Dad never wanted me to have friends and now I know why."

No answer for that. Neither Kerry nor I spoke.

"I guess I couldn't keep on staying here?"

"Oh, honey," Kerry said, "I don't think that's possible."

"I know. But I thought I'd ask anyway."

"It's not that we don't want you . . ."

"I know," Emily said again. "Is it all right if I go to my room now?"

"Of course it's all right. Would you like to take Shameless with you?"

"No. I want to be alone."

"Well, if there's anything . . ."

She shook her head and got up and went away, small and stooped, very young and very old.

Kerry and I just sat there. After a while she said, "My God, that was awful. Awful. The look on her face . . . I wish there was something we could do for her."

"She can't keep on living here. You know that."

"I know it, but still . . . something . . ."

"We already did the only thing we can do," I said. "We told her the truth."

Cybil paid us a semisurprise visit two nights later. She'd been asking about Emily and she wanted to meet her and she didn't care to wait, she said, until we got around to issuing an invitation or bringing the kid to Larkspur. She didn't drive much anymore, especially at night, which was a measure of how deeply her interest ran. Besides which, it was obvious she was still feeling her oats; the Nurse Dunn episode and the attendant publicity had elevated her confidence level and made her a touch more imperious.

There was an instant rapport between Cybil and Emily. The girl had been quiet and withdrawn, keeping mostly to herself, but Cybil's arrival seemed to perk her up some. The two of them shut themselves up in Emily's room for a private get-acquainted session which lasted more than half an hour. When Cybil came out, alone, she had a sharp little gleam in her eye. She perched on the sofa, looked at Kerry, looked at me, and said, "Well? Are the two of you going to do the right thing by that child?"

"What kind of question is that?" Kerry demanded. "We are trying to do what's best for her — "

"Don't be dense. You know what I'm talking about."

"I don't know."

"Adoption. A-d-o-p-t-i-o-n."

I said, "What?"

Kerry said, "We couldn't do that."

"Of course you could. You've talked about it, surely?"

"No, we haven't."

"Well, you've each thought about it, and don't try telling me different. It's what the child wants, you know that."

"Did Emily tell you it's what she wants?"

"She didn't have to put it into words. It's in her eyes and the way she talks about the two of you. She needs a mother and a father. A grandmother, too, for that matter." Cybil fixed Kerry with a steely eye. "I've been denied that privilege so far and I'd like to be one for a little while before I croak."

"Mom, for heaven's sake . . ."

"Hah. You haven't called me Mom in years. I like hearing it. I'd like hearing Grandma even better."

I said, "You might as well forget it, Cybil. It's not going to happen."

"Why isn't it?"

"For a lot of reasons. I'm nearly sixty and that's too old — "

"Nonsense."

" — to be an adoptive father, even if the courts would allow it. I'm too set in my ways, that's another thing. So is your daughter."

"Nonsense, I say."

"Plus, I have a sometimes dangerous profession, and Kerry and I both work odd hours and there are nights when neither of us gets home until late, if we get home at all."

314

"Not an issue. There are private schools, nannies, sitters. And me, in a pinch."

"We can't afford private schools or people to come in — "

"Horse apples. Don't you think I know what the two of you earn in a year, how much you have tucked away?"

"Cybil, listen to me — "

"I will not. You both care about the girl, any fool can see that, and she cares about you. That's what matters. That's *all* that matters."

"We are not going to become parents. We couldn't if we wanted to. The child welfare people, the courts — "

"Damn all that," Cybil said. "If you really want to adopt that little girl, you can find ways and means to do it. And I think deep down you do want to, both of you. You'd better give it some serious consideration. I mean that. Serious consideration."

All right, so we gave it some serious consideration.

The answer was the same: No.

We talked to Emily about it, tentatively at first, then openly. Kerry's idea. It was what the kid wanted, all right. No begging, no pleading, just the big soulful eyes and a small hopeful smile.

The answer was still no.

Tamara, naturally, thought it was a splendid idea.

No.

The social worker who came to talk to Emily and to Kerry and me didn't rule it out.

No.

Cybil kept calling up and lobbying.

No.

Kerry went to see a family lawyer she knew. He thought it could probably be managed, given the unusual circumstances and despite our ages, if all parties were in accord and the judge in the case was the sympathetic type.

No.

Then one evening while I was dozing in my chair, Emily came and sat on the arm and looked at me and then snuggled down and laid her head on my shoulder.

Just say no and keep on saying it.

But dammit, I'm not made of stone . . .

The employees of Thorndike Press hope you have enjoyed this Large Print book. All our Large Print titles are designed for easy reading, and all our books are made to last. Other Thorndike Press Large Print books are available at your library, through selected bookstores, or directly from us.

For information about titles, please call:

(800) 223-1244

To share your comments, please write:

Publisher
Thorndike Press
P.O. Box 159
Thorndike, Maine 04986

X